Gannon's Law

When Sheriff Jim Gannon's wife-to-be, Kate, is gunned down by a sniper it triggers off a chain of events that brings the lawman into bitter conflict with bullying Jack Clayton and his sons. Gannon is drawn into a web of treachery, robbery and murder involving stolen Union gold and a mysterious renegade Confederate soldier – Clay McIntire.

Only after tracking down the outlaw gang and learning of their secret past does Gannon realize that his life is in danger from friend and foe alike.

But does the knowledge come too late?

Gannon's Law

PETER WILSON

A Black Horse Western

ROBERT HALE · LONDON

© Peter Wilson 2009
First published in Great Britain 2009

ISBN 978-0-7090-8783-0

Robert Hale Limited
Clerkenwell House
Clerkenwell Green
London EC1R 0HT

www.halebooks.com

Typeset by
Derek Doyle & Associates, Shaw Heath
Printed and bound in Great Britain by
CPI Antony Rowe, Chippenham and Eastbourne

ONE

Jim Gannon pulled the star from his shirt and threw it into the open drawer of his office desk. It had been a bad day and his mood was as sour as the stale coffee.

He had stood helpless and disbelieving as the Clayton brothers – guilty as hell of the murder of the harmless old Zeke Bannister – had walked out of the courthouse laughing and joking and heading straight for the saloon to celebrate. They had even offered Gannon a mock salute as they strode out into the afternoon sun.

Self-defence. That had been their case. And although it was true that the old man had been found clutching a gun, Gannon knew for certain that he had never fired a pistol in his life and his gnarled old fingers would have been useless. He knew that the Claytons had used Bannister for sport. The town knew it, and the judge knew it but still the brothers walked free on the evidence of an eye witness, a drink-sodden Mexican, Carlos Suarez, who would sell his sister for a dollar.

Gannon never knew how much Jack Clayton paid Suarez to provide the evidence that would give his boys their freedom but he knew that the old man was not known for his generosity. Meanness of spirit was part of the Clayton stock and Suarez would have come cheap.

Gannon pulled a face as he took another sip of the coffee.

'D'you get the water for this coffee out of the horse trough, Ned?' Gannon said as he unbuckled his gunbelt and threw it across the back of his chair.

Young deputy Ned Hilton grinned. The sheriff always complained about the coffee but he went on drinking it just the same.

This time, though, Ned knew that Gannon's mood had nothing to do with the taste of the coffee. He had watched from the office window as the two killers – like Gannon he knew what to call the Clayton boys – walked free from the courtroom and headed for the Nugget saloon.

'You did your part, Sheriff,' he said hoping to lighten the gloom. It was a vain attempt.

He knew how much law and order meant to a man like Jim Gannon. He had been sheriff of Springwater for little more than three years. Ned had been an idealistic youth with romantic ideas of law and order when Jim took his oath for the first time and in the first two years in office he had kept Springwater a clean law-abiding town.

Then the Claytons had moved in and they had been trouble almost from the first day.

Jack Clayton, his wife Ruth and sons Billy and Ike had taken over the Clarke place five miles out of town after the death of Ruth's father Josh Clarke. Josh had fallen from his horse and broken his neck while leading a round-up. His mount had been spooked and bolted, throwing old man Clarke clear. He hit his head on a rock and had died in the arms of his foreman.

That had been little more than a year ago when the Clarke place was a successful middle-sized ranch and a friendly neighbour. Now, under the Claytons, it was quickly turning into a run-down ramshackle place of peeling woodwork and rotting barns.

The Claytons were not ranchers.

They were drinkers and gamblers.

They were trouble.

Shootings, robberies and beatings had become part of life around Springwater and although Gannon and his team could never prove anything, the fingers of suspicion pointed at Clayton and his sons.

Nothing could be proved ... until they had gunned down old Zeke Bannister behind the blacksmith's after another drunken night in the Nugget.

But on the day of the trial the evidence suddenly

vanished. Witnesses, so sure of what they had seen on the night, became less certain, stories that old Zeke had been threatening the brothers all day started to circulate and then along came Suarez to swear that he had seen everything – that Bannister had stepped out of the darkness and called Billy's name, aimed his pistol at the young man, leaving the Clayton boys with no choice. They swore that they didn't even know it was Zeke Bannister.

'If we'd known it was the old man we would have just frightened him off,' Billy had said from the witness chair.

The look of innocence on his young face was enough to persuade some people in the room of his sincerity.

The judge, having listened to the Mexican's evidence, cleared the brothers.

It was a verdict that had sickened the sheriff and the people of Springwater who had crammed into the courtroom hoping to see their unwelcome neighbours get what was coming to them. The hangman's noose.

Gannon drained his coffee mug, grimaced again at the taste and was about to leave his office when the door opened and in walked Jack Clayton. He was a big man with a full grey bushy beard, thick brows over deep-set eyes. He more than filled the sweat-stained shirt that strained under the bulge of his huge shape. He made an effort at a smug smile but it was not returned by either Gannon or his young deputy.

When Clayton spoke his voice was little more than a gravelled croak following years of tobacco and cheap whiskey.

'Called in to say it was nothin' personal, sheriff. You had a job to do – no hard feelings on my part.'

He stretched out a hand which Gannon ignored.

'Oh, it *is* personal, Clayton. Your boys gunned old Zeke Bannister down just for the fun of it and you bought that drunken Mexican to lie. You know it – I know it – even the judge knew it. The whole town knows it. As for hard feelings – you and yours can go to Hell.' His voice rose as the anger grew but Clayton let the satisfied smile linger on his lips.

'That's no way for a lawman to talk – not after the judge has cleared my boys.'

'Your boys are as guilty as Hell and one day they'll get what's coming to them. I'll see to that. You haven't seen the last of me.'

The smile suddenly vanished from Clayton's grey face. 'Is that a threat, Sheriff?'

Gannon tried to keep his temper in check but he failed. 'You bet your life it's a threat, Clayton. Just keep those two killers away from me or you'll find yourself paying out good money to the undertaker to bury them.'

Jack Clayton's pretence that his visit to the lawman's office was an attempt to make peace disappeared.

Angrily, he snapped back. 'My boys are worth ten

of that old man, Gannon. Sure, they got out of control, they'd been drinking and, yeah, everybody knows what happened that night. But Billy and Ike have been cleared and if you've got any idea of coming after them you'll have me to deal with first.

'I ain't gonna let no lynch-happy lawman take my boys. Remember, Gannon, I don't take kindly to being ordered about.'

He turned and left, slamming the door behind him.

Ned rose from his chair and walked to the window to watch Clayton stride across the main street and into the Nugget Saloon.

'Now you've made him real angry, Sheriff, but I guess you know what you're doing,' he said.

Gannon slumped into his seat. 'No, Ned. I didn't make Clayton angry. He was born that way. And his sons were born bad. And, no again' – he grinned – 'I don't think I do know what I'm doing.'

Gannon reached up, lifted the woman by her waist and lowered her down from the buggy and into his arms. He kissed her lightly and then put his arm around her as they strolled towards the gently flowing creek that gave the town of Springwater its name.

The day after the Claytons' trial had dawned warm and sunny, the perfect morning to get out of town and away from the sheriff's office. At his side, slim-waisted but only a few inches shorter than himself, was Kate Cameron, widowed daughter of the town's mayor and the woman he had planned to marry . . . until yesterday. Now he was unsure, not of his devotion to Kate, but of his own future as sheriff of Springwater.

Gannon had seen guilty men walk free from court before and he thought he had learned to live with it. But none had been like the Claytons and as they celebrated their freedom his doubts grew. Could he carry on as a lawman? Or could he even see a future as a citizen of Springwater. He had lived there for barely three of his 36 years but Kate, on the other hand, was a pillar of local society.

She had been born in the town and in addition to being the daughter of the mayor, she was the highly-respected local schoolteacher and, more surprisingly, editor of the *Springwater Sun and Sentinel* newspaper. She had a lot to lose by leaving the town. If he decided to move on, could he ask her to give up everything to go with him? It was a dilemma he was still wrestling with when they settled on the stream bank and stared out at the clear water as it danced over the rocks as part of its long journey down to join the river and from there on to the coast.

In the silence Kate sensed his sombre mood, a sharp contrast to the sun and warmth of the day.

'Tell me about it,' she said, clutching his hand. 'It might help.'

Gannon let out a wry chuckle. 'There's no foolin' our newspaper lady, is there?' He usually called her

11

'our schoolteacher' so she sensed that this was more than just the aftermath of a bad day at the office.

'Is it the Clayton trial?' she probed. It seemed a fair guess. Since their arrest, his normal duties as sheriff had involved nothing more than locking up the odd drunk or chasing after street brawlers and trouble-stirring young tearaways.

Gannon thought briefly about the question before answering. And it was not the answer she was expecting.

'I'm thinking of turning in the badge. Of walking away,' he said, not looking at her, instead staring into the waters lapping at their feet. Stunned, Kate waited for him to say more.

'The Clayton verdict. That was only part of it, Kate.' He related the visit of Jack Clayton to his office, of how there could never be a truce between the two men. Worse, it could even develop into an open feud. 'I've tried to be an honest sheriff, to do things right and keep the law. Keep Springwater a safe place. But to see two killers walk free; to celebrate getting away with killing a harmless old man, I don't think I want to go on.' He paused, then added: 'Not here. Not in Springwater.' She studied his face, lined with a deeply furrowed brow, dark blotches beneath his usually clear blue eyes.

'I don't understand. You want to leave here? It's your home, Jim. It's our home.'

'That's right,' he said hurling a loose stone into the water. 'But what kind of home – what kind of

12

town – is it that lets the likes of the Claytons walk free in its streets? What sort of place is it to bring up children?'

Before he could stop himself, Gannon blurted on: 'This is not the place for us, Kate. Not if . . . not if we are to marry and have a family.'

They had been walking out for almost a year and it was the first time he had mentioned marriage or children. It was the first time he had said anything about a long-term future together.

He waited for her reaction but it came slowly.

'But it's our home,' she repeated as though that were some sort of solution to his problem. 'I don't know if I'm ready to – to give up all of it because of the Claytons.'

Gannon rested his hands on hers. This was not going according to plan. He had not intended to spring marriage on her. It had just come out. He had never felt comfortable in the presence of women but Kate was not like the others. For the first time he felt he wanted to spend a lifetime in a woman's company. He had never questioned her about her marriage to Dan Cameron or the circumstances of his death at the hands of some drink-crazed gunman who had escaped capture.

'I just want you to think it over—'

All talk of marriage, childen and a life together were shattered in an instant . . . the distant crack of a rifle and a bullet that ripped through the heart of Kate Cameron.

Another shot . . . this time the bullet was wide of its target, splashing harmlessly into the stream.

As the horror of what was happening hit him, Gannon clutched the woman to his chest and scrambled for the safety of the only cover available, the nearby buggy. He knew instantly that Kate had died in his arms, not because she was Kate Cameron, schoolteacher, mayor's daughter or newspaper owner.

She had been killed because she was in the company of Sheriff Jim Gannon.

The first bullet had been meant for him – the second shot confirmed that.

Tears filled the deep blue eyes of the grief-stricken lawman as he lowered Kate's body gently to the ground, as if rough handling would have caused her more pain.

But as her sightless eyes stared up at him Gannon was suddenly overwhelmed with an all-consuming anger. Who was out there? Who was skulking high on the distant hills?

Peering through the spokes of the buggy wheels he tried to focus on the area from where the shots had been fired. At first he saw nothing. Then—

There he was! To the left of the ridge . . . the glint of metal in the sun. Then a figure, crouching, seeking the cover of a bush.

Gannon returned the fire but he knew it was

useless. The killer was well out of range of his Colt
.44 but still he fired off the shots in desperation.

The mystery killer returned the fire, this time on
the run as he scampered towards his horse,
mounted up and headed out of sight beyond the
ridge.

Gannon reholstered his six-gun and looked down
at the lifeless body of the woman he had hoped to
marry.

As he fought back more tears he could not stave
off the growing feeling rising inside him. Hate and
vengeance overwhelmed him. Who wanted him
dead? Who hated him so much that they were
prepared to kill an innocent woman if she just
happened to be in the way?

The name of Clayton immediately sprang into his
mind but Gannon knew he had crossed many more
lawbreakers than the Claytons.

As he lifted the body of Kate and placed her
gently into the back of the buggy he swore to
himself that he would not rest until he had brought
the killer to justice. And as he clipped the reins into
the rear of the horse and swung back towards town
he knew that, for once, justice and the law were not
the same.

His career as sheriff of Springwater was over.
From now on he was a man on a mission of revenge.
Gannon's law was all that concerned him now.

TWO

The two men, sombrely dressed in black coats, turned away from the graveside, replaced their hats and walked side by side slowly and repectfully out of the cemetery and down the hill towards the town. Neither had spoken for several minutes, both acknowledging that the other's sense of loss was just as painful as his own.

Henry Logan had lost his only daughter while his companion had watched his wife-to-be die at the hands of a distant rifleman. Both men were grieving and hurting.

The silence continued until the pair reached the imposing building at the edge of town ... the Springwater Banking and Trading Company owned by Mayor Logan. Also housed in the two-storey, brick-built block was the *Springwater Sun and Sentinel* newspaper.

'This was her pride and joy,' Logan said at last, more to break the silence than to make any useful

observation. 'A successful woman newspaper owner
– there can't be too many of them.'

'Suppose not,' Gannon agreed. He was in no
mood for small talk but every man had his own way
of dealing with the loss of a loved one. 'What will
you do with the paper now?'

Logan shrugged. 'Sell it. Close it down. Who
knows? Right now I'm not too sure of anything.'
Then, fighting back more tears, he added: 'She'd
have made you a good wife, Jim.'

Gannon rested his hand on the older man's
shoulder.

'I know that, Henry. We both know that Kate was
as good a woman as any man could hope to have for
a wife.'

'Who would do this, Jim? Who would kill an
innocent schoolteacher like Kate who never did
anybody any harm in her whole life, not even that
snivelling wretch Dan Cameron.'

It was the first time Henry Logan had mentioned
his daughter's first husband. All Gannon knew
about him was what Kate had told him about his
death at the hands of a drunken cowboy one night
some four years ago, well before Gannon's arrival in
town. And the only memory of him was the
photographs she had shown him. One was of the
two of them posing together. Smiling. The other – a
full-on face of the man she had married.

Gannon had little interest in Dan Cameron on
this day of Kate's funeral. The two days that had

17

passed since her death had not lessened his resolve for revenge. Or his decision to turn in his sheriff's badge. He had not been able to bring himself to tell Logan that Kate's death was truly a murder of the innocent, that the rifle bullet had been intended for him and she had simply been in the wrong place at the wrong time. And now was not the moment for the truth.

Suddenly, Henry Logan changed the subject. 'I guess you'll be leaving Springwater now and the town will be looking for a new sheriff.' Gannon had thought about that and he had decided to stay. Whoever had killed Kate and wanted him dead was still around to try again.

Jim Gannon would make himself a willing target.

'I'll be around for a few days, Henry. I'll let you know when I decide it's time to move on.'

The two men shook hands and Logan went into the newspaper building while Gannon headed down the street to the sheriff's office.

It was time to clear out his desk and give young Ned Hilton his instructions about what to do until the new man took over.

He paid no attention to the horse hitched at the rail outside his office as he mounted the boardwalk. He was just about to enter the office when the door opened and his young deputy stood in front of him.

'Glad you're back, Jim. You've got a visitor. I told him you were at a funeral but he said he knew all about that and he would wait for you. He wouldn't tell me his name. Said you'd probably guess who he was.'

Intrigued, Gannon eased the young deputy aside. 'Let's not keep him waiting any longer, eh?'

But as he stepped out of the sunlight and into the darker surroundings of the room that had been his office for three years, Jim Gannon stopped in his tracks. He felt as though he was staring into the face of a dead man.

The visitor rose from his seat and crossed the room. He had the same dark sideburns, the same closely-set eyes, pointed features above a square unshaven jaw. His smile was hidden behind a thick moustache.

'No, Sheriff, I'm not back from the dead. Matt Cameron's the name – Daniel was my brother.'

The likeness to the photograph Kate had kept on her piano was uncanny. Now, as his eyes adjusted to the dimmer light of the office, Gannon could see that Matt Cameron was slightly heavier around the jowls, a few years older and starting to turn grey around the temples. Even so, the family resemblance was unmistakable.

Before Gannon could say a word, the stranger hurried on. 'I was up in Masonville when I heard about Kate's death and the funeral. Sorry I didn't get here in time.'

'Why have you come?' Jim Gannon's tone was cool, unfriendly.

19

'Kate was married to my brother – sort of family, I suppose. Thought I ought to pay my respects.'

Gannon remained silent. All that seemed reasonable enough. Masonville was a small one-horse town a few miles north and news of Kate's murder would have reached there by way of the storekeepers who regularly used the Springwater Banking and Trading Company.

The visitor perched on the corner of the sheriff's desk. 'I wasn't just in the territory by chance. Nobody ever paid for gunning down my brother – nobody even tried to find the killer. The sheriff here before you came just said it was some drunken cowboy who'd ridden out of town before anybody could do anything. So I thought I'd try.'

He sighed heavily and then went on: 'I thought I'd hit lucky up in Kansas City a year or so back but the trail went cold.'

Satisfied that he had said all he wanted the sheriff to know he added: 'Your deputy here tells me you and Kate were walking out together – mebbe thinking of getting married.' He noticed Gannon's slight nod and added: 'I'm sorry. I liked Kate. Liked her a whole lot.'

'She was easy to like,' Gannon agreed but he was beyond thinking whether this man Cameron liked his sister-in-law or not.

He was about to turn in his badge and go in search of the killer and once he had found him, take the law into his own hands. He would not risk the chance of any judge letting the killer go free.

Now here was another man on a mission to find a killer and solve the five-year-old murder of a brother.

Two men with a common aim . . . two men whose paths were sure to cross again. And those paths would surely be stained in blood.

Cameron left the office to stroll up to the cemetery and pay his respects at the graveside before finding himself a room at the Springwater Hotel where he intended to stay for a couple of days before moving on. He was a drifter, homeless by choice since the loss of his brother. The story he had given to the sheriff was enough to satisfy him and explain a short stay in the town where he expected to uncover enough information to carry out the real reason for his visit.

Gannon began the task of clearing out his desk. It would not take long. Apart from a picture of Kate, another of his parents and a cutting from the *Springwater Sun and Sentinel,* written by Kate herself, reporting the murder of Zeke Bannister and the arrest 'by our own Jim Gannon' of the Clayton brothers, there was little of personal interest to the retiring sheriff.

He read through the newspaper report and then, slowly, deliberately, he tore the cutting into shreds and tossed them into the trash tin he kept at the side of his desk. There were memories he would like to take with him, others he wanted to leave behind.

'It's up to you now, Ned, but I'll be around for a few days if you need any help.'

With that, he took one last look around the office and stepped out into harsh sunlight. His small house stood at the far end of the main street close to the little chapel that served those members of the town that still believed they were living in a God-fearing community.

It was at the quiet end of Springwater and Gannon had the feeling that, if he decided to stay around, that was how he was going to like it in the future.

He nodded to a few neighbours who stopped to pass on their condolences at the death of Kate – their courtship had long since ceased to be any secret – and called in at the general store to stock up on a few provisions.

As he was leaving he glanced across the street towards the saloon. He didn't see the couple immediately but as they stepped out from the shade of the overhang on the boardwalk they came into full view. Although they were well out of earshot they appeared to be involved in a deep conversation. Gannon turned away and headed for his house, wondering what Ruth Clayton and the man who called himself Matt Cameron had in common.

The drunk staggered out of the Nugget and vomited into the dust. It was late and Springwater was in total darkness and silent except for the few late night gamblers at the card tables. He stumbled into a horse trough and cursed aloud. Further along he steadied himself by holding on to a hitching rail.

The night had gone well. He had told them he wanted – no, more than that, he had reminded them he was worth – a lot more money than he had been paid. He had earned it and they should show their appreciation.

They could not go around treating him like a nobody. They were the ones who were nobodies without him. They should remember that. That's what he had told them.

He slumped against the fencing of the livery. He needed to relieve himself and almost fell into the alleyway. His head was starting to ache, the result of a whole day's drinking and he groaned aloud as he leaned against the wall.

He was only vaguely aware of the approaching footsteps but he paid no attention until a voice whispered his name. He turned to see a familiar face; even in the darkness there was no mistaking the twisted grin. The drunk tried to return the smile and grunt a friendly greeting but it never left his lips. In an instant he was clutching his gut as the cold steel blade of a killer's knife was thrust deep into his stomach. As he slumped to his knees, the killer withdrew the knife and stood over the writhing figure.

He uttered just two words as he watched the life drain out of the man who had tried to betray him.

'Greedy bastard,' he whispered as he knelt to check that the other was dead and then with one swish of the blade, put the finishing touch to his night's work. Then he walked out into the main street and back to his game of cards in the Nugget. . . .

Jim Gannon was wakened by a heavy banging on his front door. The sun was up but the retiring sheriff had had a restless night, falling asleep shortly before dawn. He struggled out of his bed and bleary-eyed, opened the door to find Ned Hilton standing on his porch step. Even half-awake, Gannon could see that something was wrong.

'You said if I needed any help you'd still be around,' Ned said.

Gannon tried to smile. 'I didn't expect you to take up that offer so soon, Ned. What's wrong?'

'It's Suarez – you know, the Mexican who gave evidence in the Claytons' trial.'

'I know him,' said Jim grimly.

'He's dead, Jim. His body was found in an alley back of the livery. His throat had been cut.'

THREE

The burial of the murdered Mexican Carlos Suarez, went almost unnoticed in the town of Springwater. He had no family in town and was looked upon as no better than an objectionable drunkard. There were even those who thought he had tried to improve his popularity by testifying on behalf of the Clayton brothers at their trial.

The fact that Judge Jacob Potts had believed him and the brothers had walked free had still not convinced the townsfolk of their innocence. Now the man who had saved the Claytons from the hangman was in the ground, knifed to death in a back alley.

Gannon did not waste time attending the Mexican's funeral and even Ned Hilton's plea for help left him unmoved. He didn't care who had butchered Suarez and in other circumstances he would have felt that whoever did it had done the people of Springwater a favour.

He had his own ideas about the killing. Suarez

was a slack-tongued brute and loose talk could land a man in a whole lot of trouble. If he had been asked to give an opinion about the identity of Suarez's killer, Gannon would not have looked far beyond the Claytons.

They owed him – and it was a debt money couldn't buy. They owed him their lives and that made him dangerous to have around. The Claytons wouldn't be happy until he was silenced and that put them right at the top of Gannon's list of suspects.

As he and Ned sat eating their steaks in Ma Laker's small restaurant across the street from the jailhouse, Gannon could see that the deputy who had taken on the temporary role of town sheriff was ill at ease.

'What should I do, Jim? I can't just forget it, even though that Mex was a critter of the worst kind. Until the new sheriff takes over I'm responsible. I have to do something.'

Gannon took a long drink of his coffee before answering. Eventually he relented and said: 'If it were me, Ned – and it ain't if that's what you're starting to think – I'd try to find out what Suarez was up to before he was found in that alley. My guess is that he spent the night in the Nugget where he would be shooting his mouth off. That'll be what got him killed is my thinking.'

Ned nodded slowly. 'So, you think it was the Claytons?'

'You can count on it, Ned. But you'll need proof

– and even proof may not be enough for Potts. Remember the last time?'

The two men finished their meal and were about to leave when the door opened and the man who had been the subject of much of their conversation walked in.

Judge Jacob Potts was a mean-faced man who, despite stooping shoulders, stood over six feet tall. He was dressed in a grey suit that matched perfectly his pale thin features. He looked around the room, his eyes darting like a frightened rabbit as he searched for an empty table.

A man in his early fifties but looking much older, he was on his first visit to Springwater, one of the stopping off points of his circuit that covered a vast territory of small, insignificant little towns to the south of the state. Since the Clayton trial he had been waiting for the telegraph message that would beckon him to his next case.

Gannon resisted the temptation to challenge the judge as he brushed past the two lawmen on his way to the only vacant table.

Nothing could be changed. The Claytons were free; Kate was dead and buried; and Gannon had resigned as sheriff of Springwater. Now there was still a murderer loose in town. As the duo left the restaurant, he was still wondering whether the time had come to move on. He knew the chances of finding Kate's killer were diminishing with every passing day.

But the fates had something else in store for Jim Gannon. His days of fighting lawlessness and injustice were far from over.

Ruth Clayton was happy to see the back of the trio as they headed away from the ranch and out towards the town. Not for the first time she wondered what had possessed her to marry a man like Jack Clayton. Worse, she had found herself forced into taking in, feeding and fending for his two worthless sons.

Ike and Billy had run wild from an early age and nothing had changed in the few years their father had been married to pretty Ruth Clarke.

It had not always been like this, she remembered, not in the early days. Jack had been a man of much charm and magnetism during their courtship and even impressed her hard-headed father on the rare occasions that they visited the ranch from their home two days' ride out of Springwater.

But no sooner had their wedding vows been taken than a frightening change came over Jack.

The kind, considerate man she had married became a bully, a heavy drinker and a gambler who spent most of his time in the town. And, Ruth learned to her horror, in the company of saloon girls and prostitutes. Her husband, Ruth now believed, was merely reverting to type, that the pleasantness and charm had been a mere front.

It was a lifestyle that suited the young Claytons.

Both were handy with their fists and fast with their guns.

Ruth began to live in fear; her husband's brutality coupled with her stepsons' contempt had turned her from a loving wife and caring stepmother into a bitter woman. Several times when the men were in town she had been tempted to pack a few essential clothes, hitch up a buckboard and head for pastures new.

But each time one thing held her back – the ranch had been her family home as a child. Her father had lovingly cared for the place, just as she had done when her mother was alive. She would not run off and leave everything to the Claytons. The place had already become a run-down ramshackle shell. Cowhands, loyal to her father, had walked out in disgust at the behaviour of the new owner and his sons.

Ruth had hoped that her troubles might be over when the brothers were accused of the murder of Zeke Bannister, a harmless old man, but they had walked free on evidence that Ruth knew had been paid for by her husband. Her life was becoming a daily misery and she had to find a way out. And she thought she knew a man who would help her. It was time to let him know the secret she had been forced to keep.

Gannon had developed a gift for being a light sleeper, usually with the comfort of a six-gun under a pillow, so he heard the sound immediately. A short scraping noise of somebody trying to break into his house. Instantly alert, Gannon slid from the bed, and edged his way across the darkened room. He waited for a repeat of the sound that had wakened him. There it was again. Somebody was trying to force the lock. Silently, Gannon crept closer to the source of the noise, his gun ready. Then, just as suddenly as it had been broken, the silence returned.

He waited, puzzled. Had he imagined the noise? Or had it simply been a stray dog scratching for night food?

The answer came immediately in the form of an ear-shattering blast of gunfire. Shards of glass and wood splinters flew across the room as Gannon dived for the cover of an upturned chair. Blindly returning the fire, Gannon felt a bullet scorch his left arm before smashing into a mirror behind him.

Whoever was out there had lured him out into the open and now he was a sitting target. He knew from experience that neighbours would not come running to his rescue. They would hear the shots, peer out into the night and curse the disturbance but put it down to more drunken high spirits before returning to the comfortable safety of their beds.

Gannon, his eyes now accustomed to the darkness of the room, scrambled on all fours towards the rifle hanging in its sheath on the corner of the bed. Sliding along the floor he reached the window looking out into the alley at the back of the house from where the attack had come.

It was a moonless night and outside was pitch darkness. Gannon strained his eyes but could see nothing. There was only darkness. And more silence.

The minutes ticked slowly by without further gunfire.

Was he – were they – still out there?

Then, without warning, it was over.

Another gunshot, though this time not fired in Gannon's direction, was followed by the sound of pounding horses' hoofs and an eerie shriek from somewhere in the alley.

Gannon rose to his feet and rushed out into the night. But before he could raise his rifle they were gone, escaping along the street behind the row of small houses and the town's chapel.

He returned to the house, straightened the upturned chair and sank into its comfortable seat. Sitting in the darkness, he rolled himself a cigarette and watched as the smoke rose to the ceiling.

Jim Gannon had never been a gambling man but he would have gladly put a few dollars on the identity of the night raiders. He could never prove it but the first names that sprung to mind were Billy and Ike Clayton. But the question remained – if they had come to kill him, why had they not finished the job?

He fell into a troubled sleep still wondering. . . .

For the second night the former sheriff was finally stirred from his fitful slumbers by another noise – this time the sound of loud banging on his door. Then a shout.

'Gannon! You in there?' Another banging on the door.

Jim Gannon struggled to his feet and staggered towards the door to greet his early morning caller. Grunting at the sight of the man on his doorstep. he moved aside to let his visitor into the house.

The smashed windows, the bullet-splintered wood of the doors and furniture told the story of the previous night.

'Looks like you had some unwelcome guests last night,' said Matt Cameron, straightening one of the overturned chairs.

Gannon poured himself a glass of water from the bedside pitcher. 'You could say that. Any ideas?'

He looked closely at his visitor. Cameron was the last man he had expected to make a social call.

'Seems somebody doesn't like you much, but I'm a stranger in town these days, remember?'

Gannon let it drop. He didn't need Cameron's suggestions, especially, in view of what he had seen outside the Nugget, that they were unlikely to include the Claytons. Matt Cameron and Ruth Clayton knew each other – and for Gannon that put himself and Kate's brother-in-law on opposite sides.

'So, what brings you this way?' he asked after a lengthy silence that included an inspection of the damage.

Cameron hesitated but surprised Gannon when he eventually spoke. 'I need your help. I had a visitor last night. A lady.'

Gannon found himself chuckling. 'Do I need to know this?'

Cameron ignored the innuendo.

'Ruth Clayton came calling. She was Ruth Clarke when I lived in these parts. Moved back here with her husband and his two sons when her old man died and left her his small spread.'

Gannon waited to be told something he didn't already know. His visitor threw his hat on to the table and settled into one of the chairs.

'Ever heard of somebody called Clay McIntire?' Cameron asked.

Gannon shook his head. The name meant nothing to him.

Cameron went on, 'According to Ruth Clayton, McIntire could be the man who killed my brother; could even be the same person who killed Kate.'

'Go on,' Gannon prompted him.

'You've been in Springwater what four years—'

'Nearly three—'

'Long enough to know it's a strange town. A town with divided loyalties during the war. This is a border town that was torn between the Union and the Rebs. Even families fought on opposite sides.'

33

Cameron was suddenly friendly, almost conspiratorial. 'I don't know about your loyalties, Jim, but here in Springwater there were – still are – folks who think the war was won by the wrong side.'

Gannon rose from his chair and refilled his water glass.

'The war's been over for more than three years. It's time people got used to that.'

Cameron interrupted him: 'The fighting may be over but the hating sure as hell ain't. Or the feudin'. This is Missouri, Jim, too close to the South for some folks to forget that easy.'

Gannon wondered where this was going but Cameron took him by surprise with his sudden change of direction.

'What do you know about the Logan family?'

What was there to know? Kate was – had been – a Logan before her marriage; her father was the richest man in town and its mayor; Cameron's brother had been married to a Logan. What else was there?

'The Logans are a powerful family in these parts, Jim. You know Henry Logan, Kate's father, but he had two brothers down south in Tennessee even richer than he is and they all made their money out of the war.'

'Had? You said had?'

'Both dead now. I'm surprised Henry Logan never mentioned them. Though mebbe not, considering everything.'

Gannon sat in silence as Cameron related the story of how the Logans had played both sides of the conflict; supplying both with cannons, rifles, horses, supplies. Then, when the war started to go badly for the South, they changed their allegiance and threw in their lot with the Union.

'Meantime, Henry thinks he's safe up here in Springwater,' Cameron said quietly.

'Safe from who?' Gannon asked urgently. 'And what's all this got to do with Kate's killing.'

There was a brief silence while Cameron considered how much further he should go. He suspected that Gannon thought Kate Logan had been killed by mistake – that the gunman was really after the man who had just turned in his badge. If he was allowed to go on thinking that he might be just the ally Cameron needed.

But, if he knew the truth, if he knew that the bullet had been intended for Kate and he was just the man in the way, how would he react? Would that make him even more hell bent on vengeance – to find his woman's killer?

Cameron decided that it was time to find out and to tell the former sheriff the truth. Or at least as much of the truth as he thought would be necessary.

'The Logan brothers double-crossed a group of deserters and rebels who had broken from Quantrill but were just as violent and murderous as those bushwhackers. Mebbe not as notorious but they were led by a man called Clay McIntire. We think he's behind the killing of Kate and her two uncles. Her father is still alive only because they are saving the biggest fish for last. Henry Logan may be Springwater's number one citizen, Jim, but he was one of the family who sold out McIntire and his gang and they won't rest until they get him.'

FOUR

'Who are you?'

It was Cameron's turn to be taken off guard by a question he wasn't expecting but Gannon pressed on: 'I know you're the brother of Dan Cameron, but you're more than that. You didn't come to Springwater just to solve a four-year-old murder. Not so much, who are you – more to the point, what are you? And what has Ruth Clayton's visit got to do with this? I saw you with her outside the general store.'

Cameron shifted in his seat. He wasn't used to being questioned and this man Gannon was no fool.

'Ruth and I have known each other since we were young kids. Our families were neighbours. Our meeting in the street was a pure accident but I could see she was nervous. When I asked her what was wrong she just turned away.

'Then, last night, she contacted me again. She

wanted to know why I was in town – I hadn't been back since before the war and she had already left after her mother died. Her father sent her off to Jefferson City where he had family who ran a small business. They took Ruth on as a store assistant and that was where she met Jack Clayton. Seems everything was fine until she got a message that her father had died and the farm was hers. Ruth, Clayton, and his two sons Ike and Billy came to Springwater and took over the running of the place. Except running a small spread was not their idea of a good life.

'She had heard of Clayton's reputation up in Jefferson City but she had always found him to be charming and honourable – until they got wed.' Cameron paused, as if searching for the right explanation. Then he went on, 'The man's a drunk and a bully, Jim, and he's made Ruth's life hell. But even worse his sons are just like him.'

Gannon felt it was time to have a say. 'I know all about the Claytons. And you'll have heard that I arrested the boys for killing an old timer in town.'

Cameron nodded. 'I heard.'

'Then you'll also have heard that they walked free from the court, laughing at the law. They're killers – and Clayton's no better.'

'And that's why Ruth came to see me. She was too frightened to come sooner but when she saw me in the street, a man she had known as a kid and who'd been her first sweetheart – like I said, we were just kids – she decided to take a chance.

'Jim, she knows that Jack Clayton paid the Mexican to lie about what he'd seen; she had even heard the brothers boasting about killing that old man but she was too frightened to come forward. And, don't take this wrong, Jim, she didn't really trust you as sheriff; not with your connections to the Logans who she'd been warned about.

'But now they've struck again and this time she's ready to talk.'

'The Mexican?'

'He was shooting his mouth off in the saloon, demanding he got what they owed him. Ike made sure he did get what was coming to him a coupla nights ago.'

Gannon thought for a moment then said: 'I think you should go see Ned Hilton – he's the sheriff now.'

'Don't be a fool, Jim, Ned's only a kid himself. He can't handle this.' Then, seeing the doubts appearing in Gannon's face, he added: 'And there's more to it. Ruth thinks her husband only paid off the Mex to save his sons' hides; that he, well, he was just doing what any father would do.'

'That still makes him guilty of a cover-up,' Gannon snapped, rising from his chair.

'Oh, I think we'll find he's guilty of much more than that, my friend,' said Cameron quietly. 'Ruth reckons that last night, before she came out to meet me while the Claytons were drinking and whoring

39

in the Nugget, she heard them talking about somebody she had never heard of before. Clay McIntire. She didn't really catch what they were saying but for what it's worth she thinks that Jack may have ridden with the McIntire gang. If that's right then I'd be wagering that he isn't through with the gang just yet. Not while Henry Logan is still alive.'

Like Gannon, Henry Logan woke early that morning. Not by any banging on his door but by the recurrence of another bad dream. He had been having plenty of those lately and now the murder of his daughter brought home the realization that he, too, was living on borrowed time. Life in Springwater had been good to the youngest of the Logan brothers.

He had left the family home in Tennessee as a young man eager to make his way in the world and, though he could never admit it to them, to escape the influence of his older brothers. Henry felt he was different from them, certainly not cut out for the kind of life they had planned.

Making big money out of arms-selling during the Mexican War in the Forties, and running whorehouses, was not his idea of a good life. But he was still a Logan and when the offer came to use the brothers' money and set up a trading company, with the cover of a bank to stash away their ill-gotten gains, he didn't refuse. He became one of them.

At first, life was good. He was a respected citizen of a small out-of-the-way Missouri town, happily married with a young daughter, while his brothers continued to finance his own enterprises, including the purchase of the *Springwater Sun and Sentinel* which he passed on to his daughter Kate.

But then in '61, came the war and with it the days that changed his life. Henry had little doubt that his brothers' arms-dealing was anything but legitimate and he knew their sympathies lay in the South while his own views were more closely aligned with the Union.

Then, in the days following the Battle of Nashville in December 1864 when, despite a spirited rearguard action by Arkansas troops, more than 9,000 Rebel soldiers died, came the news he had been dreading. George and James Logan were dead. Not, as he would have hoped, in the heat of battle – but executed. And all the gory details appeared in the newspaper cutting that still lay hidden in his office safe at the bank.

First they had been shot in the head and then hung from the balcony of one of their whorehouses beside the Mississippi. Pinned to the chest of each man was an identical scribbled message: TRAITORS! GOOD SOUTHERN MEN DIED BECAUSE OF THESE RATS. There was even a signature of sorts 'M'.

He had never discovered who had sent him the information. Or why.

He was sure there was nobody who knew of his connection with the Logan Arms Company of Tennessee and as the weeks and months turned into years and nothing happened he tried to dismiss it from his mind.

He had had nothing to do with the faulty rifles and ammunition that had caused the death of a small group of soldiers in a skirmish outside the main battle arena at Nashville. Nor with the abortive bank raid where his brothers' treachery had been exposed.

Logan shuddered at the memory even after all these years. And now his daughter was dead and buried, murdered by a bushwhacker as she tried to get her life together again.

His wife had died from a fever and now he was a man alone. As he stepped down from the sidewalk to cross the street to the offices of the newspaper he owned but planned to close, he paid no heed to the man lounging against a hitching rail next to the stage depot. But the man was watching him. Very closely. And he was already plotting the final humiliation and downfall before his lust for revenge could be completed and Henry Logan, like the rest of his family, would pay the ultimate price for treachery.

Jim Gannon finished the job of straightening the room, clearing the broken glass and boarding up the hole left by the shattered window. Cameron had left him to the task – and to think over a proposition – to join forces and hunt down a killer. To Jim, the answer had been obvious and there was no hunting involved. The Claytons, brothers and father, were the culprits. He had warned old man Clayton that he would see them all behind bars.

His belief that Kate had been an innocent victim was not weakened by Cameron's theory – that Gannon was a side issue, between himself and the Claytons, and that the bushwhacker had hit his intended target – Kate Cameron, born Katherine Logan.

Nor did Cameron's unexpected revelation – that he was a retired US Army captain now employed by the government to track down the remaining members of the McIntire crew and bring them to justice – cause Gannon to change his mind.

Their crimes belonged in the war and Clayton, not some remote figure from the past, was his problem.

As far as he was concerned the Claytons were the guilty ones and this man McIntire was Cameron's – and the Government's – headache. The Claytons had attacked his home during the night; one or more of the Claytons had killed the Mexican. Who else would gain from seeing him fill a hole in the ground? And it was a murder that had given the killer a lot of sadistic satisfaction. The stab in the gut was more than enough to kill Suarez – then to slit his throat suggested that the killer wanted much more than that.

Gannon could picture the man behind the knife – Ike Clayton was a vicious cold-hearted villain who would eventually run foul of the law once too often. And Jack Clayton would not be able to buy his freedom next time.

Gannon did not need any proof to satisfy himself that the brothers had been responsible for the night raid. Even Cameron hadn't argued that point but stressed, 'You've threatened them and they want you dead . . . or at least out of town.'

As he swept up the last of the debris Gannon thought that he had a mind to let them have their way. Springwater had nothing to keep him and a return to his home state of Kansas and a job as a cowhand on the family ranch was beginning to appeal to him.

Satisfied that the house was now in as good order as was normal, he was ready to make his way to Ma Laker's small restaurant for his usual breakfast when he had another visitor. He opened the door to a stranger, a short, plump figure with a round face that looked as though it was unused to sunlight. Or smiling. The man was dressed in a long black frock coat and top hat.

'Sheriff Gannon?' The voice was a high-pitched southern drawl.

'Not any more.'

'Begging your pardon, sir?'

'I'm not the sheriff any more – you should see Ned Hilton.'

The stranger tried to smile, and failed.

'No, you misunderstand me. I called at the sheriff's office in town. It was the young man Hilton who directed me here. He said this would be a problem you could deal with.'

Gannon allowed himself a brief smile. That sounded like Ned.

'Problem? And what kinda problem would that be, Mister—?'

'Potts. Jacob Potts, circuit judge of this county.'

FIVE

The man who had said he was Judge Jacob Potts sipped at the coffee Gannon had poured as the two men sat on opposite sides of the table that occupied the newly-tidied room.

Potts was watching his reluctant host through wary eyes. Was this man, the former sheriff, telling the truth? He wanted to believe so.

'You say you received the telegraph informing you that I would be arriving in Springwater today. You agree with that, Mr Gannon?'

'Of course, I agree,' Jim snapped back. 'But then we received another, telling us that you would be arriving three days early and that we should have the courtroom prepared.'

Potts sipped again and licked his lips. The coffee was too hot.

'I – in fact nobody from my office – sent such a telegraph, Mr Gannon, and as you can plainly see I am here today as promised.'

Gannon had checked this Potts's credentials and there was no doubt he was who he claimed to be.

'Unfortunately, Mr Potts, you are now three days late.'

Potts pondered that before asking: 'You mean you no longer have the prisoners in custody?'

Gannon smiled though there was nothing humorous about the situation. 'What I mean is that they are no longer prisoners of anybody. They have been acquitted.'

He explained how the Clayton brothers had been tried and found not guilty of the brutal killing of old man Zeke Bannister on the say-so of a local Mexican, now deceased, knifed to death in a back alley.

'Then I suggest you re-arrest them, Mr Gannon. The trial itself was clearly an illegal act so I recommend you also arrest the man who said his name was Jacob Potts. Impersonating a circuit judge is a serious offence.'

He made it sound a worse crime than the murder of an innocent old man but Gannon said nothing. Re-arresting the Claytons would give him a lot of pleasure but he knew they would not surrender quietly. There might even be gunplay but he would be ready for that. In fact, if he was honest with himself, he would welcome it.

'Well, Judge, that might not be as easy as you make it sound. The Claytons won't give up their freedom easily.'

47

Potts finished his coffee and rose quickly to his feet.

'That, as the young man, Hilton, put it to me, is your problem, Mr Gannon. Let me just say that I will be at the Springwater Hotel for the next two days. After that I have urgent business upstate and will not be here for any new trial. The cards, as they say, are in your hands. Good morning.'

He turned and left without another word, leaving Gannon to consider his next move.

A visit to the rundown ranch of the Claytons was clearly near the top of his list. But so too was the arrest of the man who had conducted the bogus trial. But before either of those he had to pay a call at the sheriff's office to retrieve his discarded star and return a relieved Ned Hilton to his former duties as deputy sheriff. Now was not the time to leave town.

Jack Clayton was in a foul mood. Although he had spent the night with his favourite whore, Rosie, at the Nugget she had not been as forthcoming as usual and when they had been interrupted by a commotion down the street near Gannon's house, she had made an excuse to call a halt to their activities. That had earned her the back of his hand across the mouth but he got no satisfaction out of the rest of the night. Now, back home at the ranch house he found his two sons sleeping off another heavy night's drinking while his wife was hiding herself out somewhere and no food waiting on the table.

Rosie's failure to give him satisfaction for his money had started Clayton's sour mood and it had not improved on the hour-long ride from Springwater. What had started out as a bad night because of the woman's failure in the bedroom was not improved in the morning by the sight that greeted him on his return to the Springwater Hotel. The new guest, a short round man in black was giving the clerk the last name he expected to hear.

'I *am* Jacob Potts,' the little man insisted as the clerk passed him the register for his signature.

The clerk, clearly not the brightest of Springwater's older citizens, repeated that Mr Potts had only that morning left the hotel – and he was a tall, thin man who walked with a stoop.

Clayton, out of view behind the plant arrangement that dominated the hotel's main entrance area, listened while the stranger continued to stress that he was a circuit judge and he was in town for a major trial. Murder, no less.

The clerk looked at him in surprise. 'Another? Who's dead this time?'

Potts shook his head in mock despair. 'Does it matter? Now, where do I sign?'

Clayton slipped out of the hotel and crossed the road to the small restaurant where he knew the fake Potts – the man he had bought to conduct the trial of his sons thanks to another pay-off for a phoney telegraph – would be eating his breakfast. He had to get him out of town before Gannon or the kid deputy discovered that the judge who had cleared the brothers was an imposter.

Potts – real name Ellis Drake; real occupation travelling thespian – was unruffled by the news of the real judge's appearance.

'I feel I ought to meet the gentleman. Perhaps pick up a few ideas for my next production,' he said theatrically.

Clayton leaned closer. 'In hell, maybe. That could be where you hold your next production if you don't listen to me. I suggest that you finish your food and lose youself somewhere in those hills out there. Else I might just have to take more precautions and you wouldn't want to know what they might be.'

Ellis Drake knew it was time to leave. He had been handsomely paid and he wanted to live long enough to enjoy the money.

'I'm gone,' he said, gulping down the last of his coffee.

Clayton followed him out of the restaurant and across to the stage depot where the fake judge had hitched his horse. He watched as the man climbed into his saddle, gave the horse's rump a heavy slap to help it on its way and leaned against the hitching rail until the man was out of sight.

Then, he turned and immediately spotted the man whose days were numbered. Some day soon

Henry Logan would make the front page of his own newpaper. Unfortunately for him, he would not be around to read it.

Ruth Clayton knew it wasn't wise to be around the house when Jack came home after spending the night in Springwater. And when the brothers were drunk they were even more detestable than their father. Unable to sleep she had been reading a story by one of her favourite writers, the Englishwoman Jane Austen, when she heard the noisy arrival of Ike and Billy an hour after midnight.

There was nothing unusual in the fact that they had been drinking heavily but she sensed that they were high-spirited over something other than cheap whiskey. They staggered up the steps and into the house and flopped into two of the padded armchairs.

'Look here, Billy. It's our Ruthie. She ain't tucked up in bed with Pa like you said. She's here waitin' for us. Ain't that so, Ruthie?'

Billy Clayton looked as though he was ready to be violently sick but he tried not to show it. Ike didn't notice. Ruth did.

'You shoulda been there, Ruthie,' Ike went on, oblivious of the fact that nobody wanted to listen. 'We sure scared the shit out of that bastard, Gannon. Didn't we, Billy? Scared the shit out of him for sure.'

When Ruth said nothing he struggled out of the

chair and staggered across the room to where she was sitting at the table and snatched the book from her grasp.

'You listenin' to me, Ruthie, or are you more interested in this' – he tried to read the name on the spine of the book but gave up immediately – 'this fairy story?'

She reached up to try to retrieve the book from his grasp but, even in his drunken state, he was too quick for her.

He pulled the book out of reach and she tumbled against him. She caught the strong smell of stale whiskey as their faces almost touched.

'Hey, Ruthie! You making a pass at me?'

She grimaced and tried to move away. But he gripped her tightly, pressing her close to him. Throwing the book aside he used his free hand to grab her around the waist and pull her towards him.

'Come on, stepmomma, Pa ain't here and you know how you're itching for a younger man,' he leered, burying his face into her throat and grappling with the front of her dress.

A feeling of nausea swept over Ruth and she used all her strength to pull away from Ike's grip. As she did so, her dress ripped away in his hands, exposing her breasts to the lecherous eyes of the drunken brothers.

Suddenly Billy Clayton was on his feet.

'Leave it, Ike. What'll Pa say?'

Ike looked mockingly at his brother.

'Pa ain't gonna say nothin' except thank me, Billy. When I've finished with this whore she ain't gonna be around much.'

Pulling her dress back into place in an attempt to cover her nakedness Ruth backed away, coming to a halt as she hit the wall.

'Get away from me, you bastard!' she yelled.

'Billy,' she pleaded, looking in vain hope for the younger brother to come to her rescue. 'Stop him, Billy. Your pa'll kill him.'

Billy Clayton was trying to be as bad as his brother.

'An' what's in it for me if I stops him, Ruth? Do I get my chance in his place?'

'You bastards!'

Billy slumped back into his seat but Ike stood in front of her, his intentions still clear.

'Now, Ruthie – looks like it's time for you 'n' me to have some fun.' He moved slowly towards her and there was nowhere for her to retreat. But as she prepared for the worst she reached out in desperation for a stick, a vase – anything that she could use for a weapon.

It was as though the good Lord was smiling down on her as her fingers folded around the trigger of the old blunderbuss that Jack Clayton kept on the shelf near the door.

Alarmed, Ike stopped in his tracks as she swung the barrel of the shotgun in the direction of the advancing attacker.

'Back off!' she snapped, suddenly unaware or uncaring that her torn dress had dropped away again exposing herself to the hungry eyes of her stepson. But he had eyes for only the weapon pointed at his belly.

'Come on, Ruthie,' he pleaded, 'you ain't gonna use that. I was only havin' a bit of fun.'

Ruth scoffed. 'Well, now I'm the one havin' fun. So back off. Or I might get a hankering to use this.'

Ike tried to smile. 'Now you know you ain't gonna shoot me. What'd Pa say?'

Ruth laughed. 'You didn't seem to care much what Pa would say when you set about trying to rape me.'

'Rape? I wasn't gonna rape you.'

Ruth glanced towards Billy. He was slumped in his chair. He might even have fallen into a drunken stupor as far as Ruth could make out. Her gaze at the younger Clayton lingered just a moment too long and Ike edged closer.

'Stay where you are!' Ruth ordered. 'This thing may not kill you, Ike, but it will make a hell of a mess of your marriage prospects.'

As she spoke, Ike made his move – a clumsy lunge to grab the shotgun.

Ruth fired and the shot scattered from the funnel-shaped barrel of the old weapon.

Ike screamed and grabbed for his lower midriff. The blast and the yell of pain stirred Billy from his drunken slumber and, seeing what had happened

54

he leapt to his feet. Ruth looked on in horror while Ike writhed on the floor of the ranch house.

Billy ran across the room, knelt over his stricken brother and stared up at his stepmother.

'What the hell have you done?'

Ruth threw the shotgun to one side and ran from the house. The buggy that the brothers had left untethered after their drunken return from Springwater was only a few yards away. Ruth jumped aboard, whipped the horse into action and headed out into the night. She had no idea where she was going – as long as it was away from the Claytons.

'The silly bitch! The stupid Irish bitch!'

Jack Clayton stood at the foot of the bed where his wounded son was still writhing in pain from the scattershot of Ruth's blunderbuss and cursed again.

Billy had been sent into town to bring the local doctor but other than that, Jack had little sympathy for his son. He knew that Ruth had always been a temptation for the older brother, drunk or sober, and he had regularly caught him leering at his stepmother as she stood over a stove or swept the dust from the veranda at the front of the house.

He had listened first to Billy and then to Ike's whining explanation of the events of the previous night but he didn't believe a word of it. They had clearly banded together to concoct a story that would explain the injuries and the woman's disappearance.

They told him they had arrived home to find her much the worse for drink and cursing the whole Clayton family, including her huband, and saying how she must have been crazy to marry a man like him, with two evil sons and giving over her family home for them to run to ruin.

Then when they tried to calm her she had gone beserk and reached for the shotgun, spraying Ike with buckshot. That was the truth according to the Clayton brothers.

Blind and deaf to his wife's real feeling, Clayton had stopped short of calling his sons two spineless liars. It was far more likely that Ike had made a move and Ruth, being a good, loyal wife, had defended herself. But even if that was the truth, Ike was still his son and Ruth was responsible for the state he was in. He had to find her. And, somehow she had to be punished.

But where was she? Clayton cursed again and stormed out of the bedroom. He stood on the veranda and stared out towards the range of hills.

'Where are you, woman? Where are you?' he yelled but there was nobody to hear.

The smile on Ned Hilton's face said everything. Jim Gannon was back as sheriff and he could go back to doing what he did best, being a deputy. Or so he hoped. But Jim had other ideas and they didn't include sitting around drinking foul-tasting coffee, scrubbing out empty cells or greeting the ladies every time a stage rolled into town.

'The way I see it, young Ned,' Jim said, pinning the star back on to his shirt, 'is we've got two days to nail those Claytons' hides to the wall. That's how long the real judge Potts will be in town before he heads upstate on what he calls more important business. The phoney Potts has already checked out of the hotel and has probably left town. I think you ought to go after him.'

He saw the look on young Hilton's face. He hadn't expected this. 'Don't worry, son, you won't come to any harm. If I figure him right our fake judge is more into make-believe violence than the real thing. He'll come quietly enough.'

Another puzzled look crossed Ned Hilton's face. Jim realized he wasn't too quick so he spelled it out.

'You wonderin' where to start looking? Well, the nearest town is Masonville and my guess is that our Mister Potts will be happy enough to rest up there for a few days before he heads further out of our reach.

'He doesn't know we're on to him so he's in no hurry. All you have to do is show him your badge, tell him we'd like a word back here in Springwater about another case.'

'But what if he don't want to come? What if he knows I don't have any jurisdiction up in Masonville to make him come?'

Jim grinned. 'Then hit him over the head and bring him back!'

Ned picked up his hat and headed for the door. 'If you say so,' he muttered on his way out.

Meanwhile Jim Gannon had other things on his mind. Last night's raid on his house and the knifing to death of a Mexican in a back alley were just two of them. On top of all that he was still not sure about so-called US Army Captain Matt Cameron. What was he really doing in Springwater? And how did the man called Clay McIntire fit into all this?

He was still thinking about Cameron when he crossed the street to the Nugget Saloon. The hardened drinkers would already be in there. They would know if his theory about the Mexican stood up to close scrutiny. If he had been demanding more money from the Claytons for his continued silence that would be more than enough motive for murder. And he didn't think Ike Clayton would ever need much of a motive to satisfy his blood lust.

SIX

Ruth Clayton leaned into the creek, washed her tear-stained face, and allowed the heat of the midday sun to dry her. She had managed to patch up her torn clothing to make herself presentable in the event of running into any of her neighbours or somebody she knew from town. But so far she had met nobody.

She was frightened and hungry and, even though she was reluctant to admit it even to herself, she was on the run. How could she now go back to the house? Jack would not believe her; he would take his sons' word over hers and they had had plenty of time to collaborate on a story that would fit the situation.

And she *had* shot her stepson. True, it was to defend herself, but would that matter to a husband who spent most nights with prostitutes and who had sired two sons like Ike and Billy?

Ike was the one she believed had been born evil; Billy, being the younger, came under his influence. Even, she suspected, to the point of killing that poor man Zeke Bannister.

Cupping her hands she drank from the creek and then searched for some escape from the heat of the sun. As she slid into the cooler shade of the tree at the water's edge, she realised that this was the place that Jack and she used to come, during the days when they were a courting couple . . . the days before he went off to do his duty for the Confederacy.

Those had been long months without the comfort of his arms around her, especially while she helped run the family store in Jefferson City. It was a lonely place for a young women in love with a man away fighting a war.

His infrequent visits to see her were filled with joy and even now she was able to look back on them with happiness. She had known that Jack had been married before and had two growing sons staying with an uncle on his farm somewhere up state. From what Jack had told her, she was not much older than Ike, his elder son, and only a few years older than Billy.

'But wait till they meet you – they'll love you,' he had promised her and, laughing at the thought, he had added, 'And if they don't they'll have me to answer to.'

But that Jack Clayton – the one who had won her heart – was now only a distant memory.

She thought that the death of her father and the move to the small ranch might bring him back to being the man she had fallen in love with. Instead, things got steadily worse. When he wasn't brooding or drinking he was in town gambling and, as she had recently discovered, spending his time with women of the night.

Taking a lead from his behaviour the brothers, too, took to drink and debauchery. Ruth was left alone to cook and clean for the three men. At the same time she suffered verbal abuse from the boys and occasionally physical attacks from her husband.

Then came last night's incident and the shooting that had forced her to flee the house that had been her family home. Strange that she should find her way to this quiet little haven with all its pleasant memories. She was deep in thoughts of the happy times when Jack was a kind and considerate suitor, a lover in a uniform she was proud to have by her side.

The thoughts sent her off to sleep and she was enjoying more pleasant dreams when she was suddenly wakened by the whinnying of a horse nearby. The sun had moved round and she had to shield her eyes as she stared up at the dark shadow of the man resting his elbows on the horn of the saddle.

Jack Clayton had found his runaway wife.

The reunion was savage. Not at first. That came later.

Clayton stepped down from his horse, tied its reins to a nearby branch and walked slowly, menacingly, to where his wife was now cowering in fear.

He was smiling but Ruth crouched, edging even further into the tiny recess that she forlornly hoped would give her sanctuary.

'Thought I might find you here, Ruth,' Clayton said quietly. 'You always used to say how much you liked to come here whenever we visited. See, I remembered your favourite place. Come here. You're not afraid of me, are you?' His voice was still calm, controlled.

'I-I'm sorry, Jack,' she stammered. 'I didn't mean—'

'Didn't mean what, Ruth? Didn't mean to shoot my boy so bad that he will be no good to any woman?' His voice had changed suddenly, alarmingly. 'Or didn't mean to encourage him like you did?'

'No! That's not true, Jack—'

'So now my boys are liars as well. Look at you! Just look at you!' Without warning he reached down and grabbed her by her hair dragging her to her feet, ignoring her screams of protest; her pleas for mercy. 'I swear, Jack, I did nothing to encourage Ike. He just—'

But the brute in Jack Clayton had taken over. He was not listening. He had not believed his sons when they told him what had happened and he didn't believe it now but reason had no part in his actions.

He was shouting now. 'You ought to be grateful that any red-blooded man would want to bed you! I sure as hell don't see the attraction of a washed-up old cow.'

Dragging her along the undergrowth, Clayton ignored the squeals of pain and with one powerful heave, hurled the frightened woman into the creek.

Spluttering as the flow of the stream threatened to carry her away, Ruth struggled to her feet and tried to scramble to the bank but was forced back into the water as her husband's anger reached new levels. The first missile, a large lump of dried clay, caught her on the shoulder, knocking her to her knees; the second missed but only because she fell face down into the water.

Gasping for breath, she surfaced to find that Clayton was now standing at the water's edge and she was staring down the barrel of his six-gun. 'I should kill you for what you did,' he snarled. 'Nobody would blame me, not even that dumb sheriff, Jim Gannon. But I ain't gonna shoot you, Ruth – not yet, anyway. Not till you've seen what you did to my boy.'

He holstered his gun and turned away and walked towards his horse. He sat in the saddle and waited while his wife, her clothes weighed down by the drenching, struggled to stay on her feet making her way to her buggy at little more than a crawl. Clayton waited while she took the reins and turned her horse.

'Stay close behind me,' he said, 'and don't think

I won't put a bullet in you if you're thinking of trying to get away. I will.'

Gannon's early visit to the Nugget brought him just the sort of news he had been hoping for.

In contrast to the main street, the room was dark and almost deserted, only two of the tables occupied, one of them by a lone drinker staring dolefully into space. At the other sat two men Gannon recognized as cowhands from one of the smaller ranches around Springwater.

He remembered that they had worked for Josh Clarke and left the jobs only when they fell foul of Jack Clayton's temper. They might be worth a chat later but first he would speak to the bartender, Sam Doyle. Doyle had been working at the Nugget for as long as anybody could remember and nothing much got past his watchful eye. Sam had a smile for most of his customers and Jim Gannon was no exception. 'Mornin', Sheriff – bit early for you to be drinkin', ain' it?'

Gannon nodded and looked around the room. 'Sure is, Sam. Like it is for most folk round here.'

He nodded towards the empty tables and the silent piano.

'Don't suppose you're in here for small talk, either,' Sam went on, rubbing vigorously and then breathing on an empty whiskey glass.

'You suppose right, Sam. I'm looking for information.'

'Always happy to help the law, Jim.' Sam paused. Then, 'You still *are* the law, ain't you? Only I heard—'

'I'm still the law, Sam,' Gannon interrupted. 'My retirement lasted all of a day and a half.'

The bartender breathed on the glass again. 'Then what can I do for you?'

Gannon explained that he was interested in what had gone on in the Nugget two nights before.

'The night the Mexican got it?' Sam stopped his glass polishing.

'Was he in here?' Gannon asked hopefully.

'Sure was – full of drink as usual. Don't want to speak bad of a dead man, but, well, I'll make an exception in his case.'

'Tell me about it,' Gannon prompted.

'He was something more than just a man with a big mouth. Kept going on 'bout how the Claytons owed him big. How he was the hero for coming forward to say what he's seen the night old Zeke Bannister was killed. How they would be swinging from the gallows if he had kept his mouth shut.

'D'you know, there were a dozen fellers in here who would gladly have put a bullet in him that night to shut his mouth for good.'

It was what Gannon had expected to hear.

'What about the Clayton boys? Were they in here to hear all that?'

'Sure they were. And boy were they angry. Specially Ike. Kept telling the Mex he shouldn't be wanting a medal just for coming out and tellin' the truth about what he saw.'

Sam picked up another glass and started to polish it while Gannon waited for the next useful piece of information. It came when the barman added, 'What was the truth? Suarez laughed in his face and I ain't never seen anybody laugh in Ike's face before. I tell ya, Jim, I ain't seen Ike so angry in a long time.'

Gannon had the feeling that Sam Doyle was not finished yet.

'What happened then?'

'That's the strange thing. Nothing much. Ike just pushed the Mexican away and told me to fill up the greedy bastard's glass – that's what he called him, a greedy baastard – for his one last drink.

'That's what he said – one last drink. Anyway Mex must have got the message because he left a short time later. Next thing we know he's lying in the alley across the street, his gut torn open and his throat cut.'

Gannon asked: 'Did Ike follow him out?'

Sam paused and rubbed his glass furiously before answering.

'Now that, I can't honestly say I noticed. By then Lily was at the piano singing and you know I've only got eyes for her when she's on the floor.'

Gannon decided to push his luck. 'Go on, Sam, you can tell me. I've only got two days to find who killed the Mexican. Then the judge is off to other business upstate. And I guess we couldn't hold them too long.'

'We-ell, I – look, Jim, this didn't come from me and I'll swear I never even spoke to you if you say it did. Yeah, Ike left a few minutes later. I thought he'd gone to relieve himself cos he was back in a couple of minutes.'

Two minutes! That was all it would take to cross the street, plunge a knife into a man who was too drunk to defend himself and be back at his table before anybody noticed.

'Thanks, Sam. That's all I need to know. Be seeing you.'

The barman replaced the now sparkling glass on the shelf and took down another.

Neither he nor the sheriff had noticed that they were wrong about nobody being around to listen to what was being said. The Nugget's handy man, old Charlie, had overheard every word. But nobody ever noticed Charlie Hodge.

He was part of the woodwork.

Still unnoticed, he took off his stained apron, put down his mop and crept into the back of the saloon. He thought the Claytons might be more than a little interested to hear that they were being talked about by the sheriff. Interested enough to pay a few dollars for the information. Charlie felt he could do a lot with a few dollars to top up the measly wage that Sam Doyle paid him for helping out.

Ellis Drake smiled to himself. It had been his finest – and most rewarding – performance, playing the role of a circuit judge with the preposterous name of Jacob Potts.

Why should he care that the man he had set free for the murder of some old town drunk had actually been guilty? His part had not been to look for reasons but simply to act out his lines convincingly and be extremely well paid for it. It had worked out well for all concerned, except poor Bannister, of course, but sentencing a young man – no matter how arrogant – to hang wouldn't bring the old man back to life. No, Ellis Drake was feeling extremely pleased with himself. He had even been able to sell his horse for a tidy sum and now he sat in his seat on the boardwalk outside the small general store in Masonville waiting to board the stage to Kansas City for the next step of his theatrical career.

Actors of his standing would be more appreciated by city folk. There his audience would consist of seasoned theatre goers, versed in the works of William Shakespeare. They would know a good Lear or Henry V when they saw one.

Drake's self-congratulatory daydreaming almost cost him his freedom. At first he had failed to notice or then recognize the lone rider making his way along the centre of the main street.

The strong sun was clearly in the rider's eyes as he scoured the street and its sidewalks for something . . . or somebody. It was only when he was a few yards away that Drake recognized and remembered the face of the deputy sheriff of

Springwater, the young man who had stood at the rear of the courtroom keeping the crowds in order during the trial. And the actor knew instantly that the young lawman was not visiting Masonville on a social call.

And, more to the point, what possible business could he have in town other than to track down a judge he now knew to be an imposter? Something must have happend back in Springwater to alert the law.

Hurriedly, Drake slipped out of his chair and moved inside the store to watch the man from Springwater dismount outside the marshal's office and, after a swift look along the street, go inside.

Again Drake allowed himself a smile. What could the deputy hope to find out from the local lawman? Nobody knew him here. The deputy knew him only as Jacob Potts and he had mischievously used the name Hamlet Macbeth to the ignoramus who was the hotel clerk.

Even if the marshal could remember seeing a likely stranger in town, by the time the deputy had asked around all the likely boarding houses and hotels, he would be aboard the Kansas stage.

No, he reflected, there was no need to worry about the witless young deputy.

Another self-satisfied smile and a nod to the storekeeper and Ellis Drake stepped out into the sunlight just as the deputy went into the saloon on the opposite side of the street.

'You certainly won't find me in there, young man,' Drake said aloud, picking up his bag and boarding the stage which was now almost ready to leave. . . .

It was more than two hours later after checking everywhere he could think of that Ned Hilton learned that the only visitor matching his description had left town on the afternoon stage bound for Kansas City. Ned mounted up, thanked the marshal for what little help he had offered, and swung his horse back in the direction of Springwater.

He had failed to find his man and he did not know what Jim Gannon would say when he gave him the news. But he didn't expect him to be pleased.

Jack Clayton's anger had not subsided. The ride home from the hideaway where he had found his errant wife had allowed his rage to fester and he had ignored Ruth's sobs and pleas as she followed close by in the buggy. Not a word passed between them on the journey and he had banished her to a locked room to fret over what further punishment he was planning for her.

Upstairs in another of the back rooms Ike was recovering from the buckshot wounds after they had been dressed by Doc Miller.

Then came the visit from old Charlie Hodge, the odd job man at the Nugget. He had brought some useful information that Gannon had his sights on Ike for the murder of the Mexican.

Clayton didn't doubt for a minute that Ike had knifed the witness after he had been shooting his mouth off in the saloon but he wasn't going to let Gannon or any lynch-happy judge have him. Just like before, he would see to it that Ike escaped the law. Only this time it would have to be different. He couldn't go out and find himself a fake judge to hear the case every time one of his sons got into trouble.

This time there would be no arrest; no courtroom. If Gannon was coming to collect Ike he would be disappointed. Ike wouldn't be there. Even before the stupid fool had tried to have his way with Ruth, Jack had big plans for the brothers – plans that would make them all rich and get the revenge he had been seeking for years.

Then Gannon could go to hell.

But first things first, he had to find a hideaway for Ike before Gannon got his hands on him. Billy would have to go too.

Jack Clayton climbed the stairs and headed first for the bedroom where he had locked his wife. It was time Ruth did her duty as a loving wife. If Clayton's plan succeeded she would not get another chance.

SEVEN

Jack Clayton hitched up his pants and made his way along the corridor to his son's bedroom. His mood had been changed by the last hour in Ruth's bed. Power had always done that for him – made him feel good. During the war he had had all the power he needed: a captain in the Confederate Army; a born leader, ruthless when needed but loyal to the men in his command.

It had been a good war for Clayton even – or especially – after the South surrendered.

What had made him a hero for the cause for four years – the robberies, massacres, the attacks on the border townships – had made him an outlaw the minute that bleating coward Jefferson Davis signed the agreement.

The official end of the war had not marked the end of Clayton's activities or the rewards that came with them. If the Confederacy couldn't have the spoils of war they sure as hell wouldn't be handed back to the Yankees.

But still it was not all finished and the time was fast coming when it had to be done.

These were the thoughts filling Clayton's head as he stood at the side of the bed. Billy was perched on the edge and Ike sat huddled against the wall, wrapped in blankets, his face contorted with a mixture of pain and anger.

Jack eyed his elder son and for a brief moment wondered if he was even worth saving from the law. Ike had always been more of a handful than his brother ever since their mother was killed, caught in a crossfire during a bank robbery.

She had been killed by a sheriff's bullet and Ike, loading up the buckboard outside the general store, was a witness. He had built up a long-standing hatred for the law and lawmen ever since.

He had gunned down one of the bank robbers and was turning on the sheriff when Clayton rushed out of the store and knocked him off his feet.

But when the sheriff, horrified at the sight of the woman dead in the dust, tried to offer his sorrow and thanks, Ike had simply spat in his face. He had been only 16 years of age – Billy was twelve – and in the eight years since that incident Jack had had problems controlling the boys. He hoped that his marriage to Ruth might change all that and bring some stability to their lives but if anything the boys, especially Ike, had become even more of a rebel. He was, Clayton knew, out of control.

But he was still his son and as he watched Ike crouching in the corner, Jack realized that the young man was vulnerable. For the first time in his adult life he needed help. He turned to the younger brother.

'Billy, I want you to go outside and hitch up a buggy. Ike and me, we've got things to talk about.'

Bemused, Billy frowned but said nothing and he obeyed what he knew to be an order. He went out, leaving his brother and father to 'talk about things'.

Jack waited until his younger son was out of the room before speaking. 'You're in big trouble, son, and this time you can't buy your way out of it.'

'What d'you mean, Pa. I told you – she made a move for me.'

Even in his state of distress, Ike Clayton had lost none of his belligerence.

His father smiled mirthlessy.

'I don't believe that and you don't expect me to believe it, either. 'Sides, I ain't talking about Ruth. You got what was coming to you.' He paused, then added, 'Can't say the same about the Mexican.'

Ike remained silent. There was no point in denying it. His father had guessed – or already knew – what had happened in the alleyway.

'That man helped to keep you from getting a noose round your neck. What you did—'

'He was shooting his mouth off,' Ike interrupted, 'If I hadn't shut it for good he'd have—'

'What, Ike? Asked for more money. I know that,

but you're a fool, son. There were better, safer, ways of keeping his mouth shut than sneaking out of the saloon as soon as he'd gone.'

It was Ike's turn to chuckle. 'What better way than slitting his greedy throat?'

'And I suppose you think nobody saw you go after him, huh?'

Ike looked away to avoid his father's accusing gaze. 'Sorry, I didn't think of that,' he mumbled.

Jack Clayton did his best to keep his rising temper in check.

'That's it, Ike. You don't think. It's what gets you into all this trouble, and now I have to get you out of it again.'

He sagged into the space on the corner of the bed vacated by Billy. 'Lucky for you, son, I do the thinking and right now I'm thinking it's time you moved out. That's why I sent Billy out to load up a buggy.'

Ike tried to sit up straight but winced at the sharp stabbing pain in his stomach.

'Run out? When did we run away from anything, Pa?'

Jack Clayton rose from the bed.

'Now, you listen to me, Ike,' he snapped. 'From here on, you do as I tell you. And right now, I say you're leaving here. That Sheriff Gannon's no fool. He's been asking around and he'll be coming to get you, so if you want to add a sheriff to your list and have a whole posse and lynch mob chasing you then stick around. You got away with killing the town drunk and nobody's gonna miss that no good Mexican but if you start messing with the lawman you're on your own.'

'Fine, Pa, whatever you say,' Ike said lapsing into a sulk.

Satisfied, Jack Clayton then turned on the sympathy.

'Look, son. I know you've had it tough since your mother died and with me being away in the war, and I know you resent Ruth.' He paused to wait for a reaction. There was none. Ike knew better than to smear his stepmother only minutes after his father had left her bed. But his time would come. She could count on that. He'd make her pay, the crazy cow.

'So – what you got planned?' he asked at last.

Clayton did not get the chance to provide his answer before Billy came rushing breathlessly into the room.

'Pa, looks like we got visitors. The sheriff and his deputy are at the gate.'

Gannon and Ned Hilton paused at the broken-down gate that opened on to the Clayton spread. The wooden nameplate with the inscription 'Clarke's' had long been torn from its hooks and cast aside in the dust but not replaced.

It was the first evidence that the place had been allowed to decline from a small but working ranch owned by Josh Clarke into the ramshackle mess it had become since the Claytons moved in. Everywhere there were signs of neglect and the few hands that had stuck around for a while in loyalty to Ruth had long since left the place to the new owners.

Gannon mopped his brow and looked around at the barren landscape with its broken fences and abandoned and rotting wagons. Briefly, Gannon remembered his own family farm in Kansas and knew how his father and brothers would flinch at such a sight. But he was not here to pass judgement on the Claytons' failure as ranchers, this was lawman's business.

Ned already had his instructions – keep his eyes peeled but let Gannon do all the talking.

As the pair rode slowly towards the house Gannon spotted Billy hitching a horse to a loaded rig. He looked up to see them approaching, dropped what he was doing like a hot branding iron and rushed up the steps to hurry inside.

'Won't need to announce ourselves, Ned,' said Gannon grinning, 'Billy'll do that for us.'

They dismounted at the bottom of the steps leading up to the house but got no further before Jack Clayton appeared in the doorway and stood blocking their path. He stood with his thumbs in his belt, his legs astride and from where Gannon was standing at the foot of the steps, looked even wider than usual.

'Sheriff. What brings you out this way? Thought we'd said all that needed saying last time I was in town.' It was hardly a warm neighbourly welcome but Clayton wasn't one for life's pleasantries.

'Like I said then, Jack, you hadn't seen the last of me. But it's not you I'm here to see. Where's Ike?'

Clayton lit himself a cheroot, blew the first smoke before answering. 'Sounds like you still got something against my boy, Gannon. You can't let it drop, can you? What is it this time? He touch up some saloon girl the wrong way?'

'There's nothing you don't know about your sons, Jack. But it's Ike we've come to see.'

'Then you're out of luck, Sheriff. He ain't here.'

'Like I said, there's nothing you don't know about your sons so you'll be able to tell me where he is.'

Angrily, Clayton threw aside his hardly-smoked cheroot.

'Cut the clever talk, Gannon. Why do you want to see Ike.'

'Because he killed Carlos Suarez. If he hasn't told you about it let me do it for him. Ike stuck a knife in your favourite Mexican and we are here to take him in.'

Jack Clayton's cold stare didn't change.

'That's some accusation, Mister Lawman. Who says it was my son?'

'Let's just say we've got enough evidence for a trial. A real honest trial this time.'

'Then it's a pity you haven't got yourself a prisoner. Like I said, Ike ain't here.'

'Then you won't care if I take a look inside the house.'

Gannon moved to climb the steps but Clayton moved out in front of him, his bulk barring the sheriff's path.

'You sayin' you don't believe me, Sheriff?'

'Something like that. You see, the Claytons aren't known for being the most truthful, God-fearing folk around here.'

Jack Clayton stretched his huge frame even wider. He was spoiling for a fight but Gannon wasn't going to rise to the bait. Both men were wearing gunbelts but were almost chest to chest, no room between them for the freedom of movement to draw.

'Insulting us ain't gonna do you any good, Gannon. And yeah, I do care about you going inside. If my word ain't good enough for you then I suggest you turn round and get back into town for reinforcements – if you can find any among that lily-livered lot in Springwater. Sure as hell this kid ain't gonna be much help.'

'Is this your turn to threaten me, Jack?'

'I'm telling you to get off my land, Sheriff. This meeting's over.' He turned and went inside the house, slamming the door behind him. Gannon thought about his next move. He had no doubt that, if he had tried to enter the house, it would have meant bloodshed. Jack Clayton was not willing to hand over his son – exactly what Gannon had expected even before he left Springwater with Ned – and he wondered if there might be some truth in Clayton's mocking suggestion that there would not be enough townsfolk to care about the murder.

Certainly not enough to commit themselves to joining a posse to take in Ike for the murder of an unloved Mexican.

Gannon knew there was no simple solution. But he had to find an answer. He had no doubt that Ike had killed the Mexican but getting him to trial before Judge Potts left town meant that time wasn't on his side.

As the two lawmen remounted, Ned spoke for the first time.

'What now, Jim? Looks like the Claytons are holding the aces.'

Gannon rested his hands on the saddle horn, looked towards the big house and spotted Jack staring down from one of the upstairs windows.

'Then that's what we'll let them think, Ned. We're leaving but we're not going too far. Ike Clayton's in there and if my guess is right, he'll be coming out before the day's much older.

'Jack says he isn't there and he expects us back with a posse so I reckon that he's planning to move Ike out before those reinforcements get here.

'All we have to do is sit and wait.'

High on a ridge overlooking the Clayton place,

Matt Cameron lowered his field glasses and retreated into the bush that had been an ideal hiding place.

He had trailed the two lawmen from Springwater and had watched as they confronted Clayton on the steps of the ranch house. Cameron's plans had not included becoming involved in a local feud – but the killing of his brother's widow Kate Logan, who had been been due to marry the sheriff, the raid on Gannon's place by the Clayton brothers, he had no doubt about their involvement, and the information from Ruth Clayton connecting her husband with Clay McIntire, were all linked in some way. And he was caught in the middle of it.

But Gannon's problems with the Claytons would have to wait. Cameron needed to know where McIntire and his men had hidden the stolen gold.

The gold. . . .

It had been a sticky night, relieved only slightly by a cool breeze, when McIntire, two of the Logan brothers and six others gathered at the abandoned homestead.

The nine men were all that was left of the group of twenty bushwhackers who had broken from Quantrill to join McIntire's crew soon after the Lawrence Massacre in August '63.

The split had come down in Texas with Quantrill losing control of his guerrillas and the restless – and greedy – among them went their own way, forming smaller groups.

Any pretence that they were still fighting for the

Confederates' cause was abandoned the night the nine men gathered to plot their raid on the border town bank where the strong room housed the Union gold. The bullion, part of a consignment shipped from the north to pay the Union soldiers, was only making a brief stopover at the bank and by morning would be part of a well-guarded wagon train. The Logans had supplied McIntire and his men with all the information they needed – the rest was now up to them.

Under the cover of darkness, six of the men had broken into the vault while McIntire and the Logans had kept watch.

The robbery had almost been completed when, suddenly, the bank was surrounded by armed townsfolk and a group of Union soldiers. Sliding back into the darkness McIntire could only watch as his men were marched out into the street and down to the jailhouse.

They had walked into a trap – betrayed by a traitor in their midst. And as he watched helplessly while the men he had fought alongside were kicked and gunwhipped along the street, McIntire searched in vain for the two men he had stationed at the far corner of the bank, the direction from which the soldiers and the townspeople had come.

There was no sign of the Logan brothers. . . .

The six prisoners were bundled into the cells of the local jail. Armed soldiers sneered at the captives, spat in their faces and hurled insults at them with the promise that there'd be a hanging party before noon.

Outside, creeping cautiously in the darkness, Clay McIntire edged his way to within earshot as the cell doors clanged shut and heavy keys were turned in the locks.

McIntire waited, listening to the sound of muffled voices while he considered his next move. He could sneak out, ride away and probably put enough distance betwen himself and the town to make good his escape.

But they were his men in there . . . and he wasn't ready to run out on them. But what was the alternative? He could hardly kick down the door and demand the release of six prioners guarded by at least twice as many armed men.

A crouching run took him closer to the side window of the building where he paused and listened.

Inside, raised voices were becoming agitated. But then he heard something that caused him to stand stock still. His name.

'This isn't the lot. There's another one out there. Clay McIntire. We told you – he was the one you had to get. He's the one the Army want . . . not this gang of nobodies you've got locked up. You've gotta get men out there and find him.'

The voice was raised in anger, becoming almost incoherent as the rage mounted. It was also instantly recognizable as that of George Logan. McIntire remained still and waited.

Inside the room there was more shouting and arguing and then, as George Logan continued his rant, several of the soldiers raced out of the building, rushing off in the direction of the bank. Somebody – not Logan this time – barked out fresh orders and McIntire risked a quick glance through the uncurtained window.

He could see the cells at the far end of the room. A

lawman was standing near a desk while two others stood with their backs to the far wall. Over to the left, George Logan and his brother were pacing up and down.

Five men in all. Six if there was another blocked from view.

The odds were never going to be better. It was now or never if McIntire was going to make any effort to free his men.

Unholstering his gun, McIntire crept to the front of the building, stopped abruptly as he almost ran into a rifle-carrying man patrolling the boardwalk.

Moving swiftly back into the shadows, McIntire pressed against the wall. The man glanced up and down the street and went back inside. McIntire weighed up his chances. Six or seven men – all but one of them armed – barred his way but not all the odds were against him. The captors had tethered the six prisoners' horses to the jailhouse hitching rail, only a few strides from the front door. Two others, belonging to the Logan brothers, were tied up nearby.

Checking again that his gun was fully loaded, McIntire made his move.

Luck was on his side. As he burst into the room, George Logan had his back to the door. McIntire wrapped his arm around the older man's throat and pressed his gun barrel against Logan's temple.

'Drop your guns!' he snapped. 'Drop 'em or I'll blow this bastard's brains all over the floor.'

He felt George Logan tremble in his grasp and he saw the fear in the eyes of his brother, standing on the other side of the desk.

84

'Do as he says!' James Logan stammered. 'He'll do it – he will.'

'You can bet your stinking hide I'll do it!' McIntire snarled. 'Now – drop 'em.' They all looked first at each other and then at the sheriff. He nodded.

'Now you!' McIntire waved towards James Logan. 'Get his keys and open those cells.' Again the sheriff nodded. 'Do it.'

McIntire waited while his men were freed. Then, dragging George Logan out into the darkness of the street, he whispered his threat: 'Don't think you've seen the last of us, you treacherous bastard! You sold us out and by Christ you'll pay for it.'

The freed men ran from the jailhouse, spotted the horses and didn't need any second orders to mount up.

'Back off!' McIntire barked at the sheriff's men as they closed in. Dragging Logan along the street to one of the brothers' mounts, he was suddenly aware of movement to his left. And the man in the blue soldier suit was aiming a rifle at his head.

McIntire pushed his hostage to the ground and fired. The soldier spun and crashed to the dirt as the bullet ripped into his chest.

Others came running, firing randomly. The sheriff and his men rushed back inside to retrieve their weapons.

McIntire dug his heels into the horse, crouching low over the saddle horn.

Over to his right he saw one of the men he had freed – then another – tumble to the ground, hit by the volley of bullets from the chasing soldiers.

Pandemonium broke out as the street was suddenly filled with angry citizens and soldiers chasing after the fleeing bank robbers. Another of McIntire's men took a bullet, this time in the shoulder, but he managed to stay in the saddle.

Behind them, the lawmen, soldiers and townsfolk were scattering in all directions as they searched for their horses to continue the pursuit. Out into the darkness, McIntire led his survivors on their race for freedom. And all the time he was still thinking of how he would make the Logan brothers pay for their treachery. With their gold. And then with their lives.

And as the shreds of the McIntire crew fled the bullets one of the two men who had crashed from his saddle as if hit by a soldier's bullet, rolled over and watched the clouds of dust from the galloping hoofs disappear into the night.

He then rose to his feet, dusted himself down, and walked back towards the town. Like the Logans, he had played his part in giving the law a chance to clap Clay McIntire in irons. That they had failed meant only that he would have to wait for a better chance to get his share of the gold.

But as he mounted his horse and headed for the safety of the surrounding hills he reckoned without the deceit of the two brothers.

While the soldiers and the impromptu posse were involved in a fruitless chase after McIntire, two men were making different plans. They knew that McIntire would never get his hands on any of the gold. It was already safely locked way in the vaults of another bank – that of brother Henry across the border in Springwater.

EIGHT

Three pairs of eyes watched as the rig and single horseman left the ranch house. Together the travellers turned towards the distant range of hills but had moved only a few yards when the rider, the bulky, easily-recognizable figure of Jack Clayton, veered off to the right, dug his heels into the flanks of the chestnut and set off at a gallop. Aboard the rig the Clayton sons kept their animal to a walking pace.

The hiding watchers waited. Up on the ridge, Cameron followed the progress of the horseman; from behind a small rock formation, Jim Gannon and his deputy Ned Hilton were interested only in the two younger men.

Gannon eased his horse into the open. This was going to be a lot simpler than he had hoped. Jack was heading off in one direction, Ike and Billy taking their rig ride south.

As he had suspected, Jack Clayton would make

sure that Ike was nowhere to be found when the sheriff returned with his hired guns to make the arrest. But Gannon hadn't assumed that the old man would leave his sons to fend for themselves.

Without his protection they were no match for a man who had handled wayward young villains all his adult life. He was just about to move off in pursuit of the rig when he spotted another rider, easing his horse down off the ridge less than a mile away.

Even at that distance there was no mistaking the identity of the rider. It was Matt Cameron and he was heading off in the direction taken by Jack Clayton.

Gannon wondered . . . but then cast the thought to the back of his mind.

He would challenge Cameron about it later.

'Come on, Ned,' he said quietly, 'we've got an arrest to make.' But he was in no real hurry. The Clayton brothers were not trying to escape – they didn't even know that they were being followed.

Gannon and Ned kept their distance as curiosity had already got the better of the sheriff. He was keen to know exactly where the pair were headed that they thought would offer them refuge. He did not know the county too well but he had the idea that the only place that could offer them any sort of hideaway was some twenty miles south and as far as he could recall, Calto had been a ghost town ever since the military detachment moved out after the war.

How long could two high-living young thugs like the Claytons hole up in a ghost town before their natural instincts for drink, gambling and women took over?

As soon as that thought struck Gannon it was followed by others. How long were they planning to stay there? Had their father already got something planned to keep them out of the hangman's clutches? And did that mean his sons would only have to go into hiding for no more than a day or two?

It was this second thought that prompted Gannon to change his tactics. Curiosity about their destination was no longer an issue. Slapping his horse's shoulders with his reins he turned to Ned again.

'Let's get after them, Ned. The sooner we lock 'em up the better. I'm getting a bad feeling about this one.'

Within fifteen minutes the two lawmen had the Clayton brothers under control, tied and silent.

Gannon had been unable to keep the mockery out of his voice as he discovered the reason for Ike's discomfort, as though he had been kicked by a bull where it hurt most men most.

But Ike found his voice at last.

'You won't hold us for long, Gannon. Pa'll see to that. I ain't done anything and you can't prove anything. You can't hold me, Gannon. You're nothin' but a small town sheriff who can't even hold on to his woman!'

It was those last words of Ike Clayton's rant that caused Jim Gannon to snap.

He spun round in the saddle, drew his gun and fired.

Ike screamed as the bullet tore into his leg just above the knee.

'You got nothing to say?' he growled, waving his gun in Billy's direction.

The younger Clayton gaped open mouthed but simply shook his head.

'Good. Because I only wounded Ike to stop him escaping and if anybody tried to tell it different I've got Ned here to say what happened.'

Ned Hilton had never seen Jim in this state but he knew the reason and he was on the man's side. He would back him all the way.

Gannon reholstered his gun.

'Right. The quicker we get you to Springwater to see the doc the less chance you got of bleeding to death, Ike.'

But as he nudged his horse into movement and headed back towards town, Gannon was not feeling very proud of himself.

Jack Clayton paused and turned in the saddle. He mopped his brow and used his hat to shield his eyes against the strong sun.

He was being followed.

At first he had paid little heed to the lone rider in

the distance but for the last hour he had deliberately ridden in circles and the man was still there, in the hills.

He had made no attempt to narrow the distance between the two and Clayton felt it was now time to lose his tail. He had business to attend to and although he would have preferred to wait until the stranger closed in and identified himself he had more important things on his mind.

His attempts to draw in his pursuer had taken up valuable time and it was still another hour's ride to the meeting place. Moving out of the sight line of the man behind, Clayton urged his horse into a gallop.

Even if the tracker did see the dust and kicked his own horse into action he would have no chance of running down Clayton before he reached the arranged meeting. Then there would be four of them to deal with the stranger and they had all come too far to let some nosy cowboy interfere.

That Yankee gold was still there for the taking and Jack Clayton was going to get his share. The wind in his face and a fast horse under him, Clayton felt a surge of the power that had been his during the final months of the war. Up ahead his men were waiting and he wasn't going to let them down.

'Aw, stop squealing like a frightened pig, you ain't hurt that bad; it's only a flesh wound.'

Old Doc Murray wiped his hands, snapped closed

his medical bag and stood up.

'You should learn to stay out of the way of buckshot and bullets,' he added with a sneer. He turned to Jim Gannon as he opened the cell door to let the medical man out. 'Sorry to tell you, Jim, but he's gonna live.'

Gannon smiled for the first time in days. 'Good – just keep him around long enough to get what's coming to him and that'll be fine, Doc. Obliged to you for coming.'

Behind them Ike Clayton was still cursing. 'I'm warning you, Gannon. You can't keep me here. I ain't done nothing.'

But Jim Gannon wasn't listening. He had heard the same thing for more than an hour, ever since he had dumped Ike and Billy in separate cells. He wasn't sure how long he could hold the younger man – probably only until Clayton came into town dragging along that crooked lawyer of theirs, Hollister, to add his legal gibberish to secure the release.

He could have Billy – but Ike was staying where he was. This time there would be no phoney judge to let him walk free from the court house. Little did he know then that the fates would again step in to conspire against Jim Gannon and force him to make a choice that would lead to even more bloodshed.

Cameron turned his horse and headed back

towards Springwater. It was clear that his quarry had spotted him and that pursuit would serve no useful purpose. But his time would come again – and then there would be no escape route for Jack Clayton.

Henry Logan rose from behind the wide oak desk that dominated his impressive office on the second floor of the Springwater Banking and Trading Company and walked across to the window overlooking the main street. He ignored the other man in the room, taking time to digest the news that his visitor had brought.

Eventually it was Sam Reynolds who broke the long silence.

'So, what are you planning to do, Henry?'

Logan shrugged. If he knew the answer to that he wouldn't be staring blankly out at the people below going about their daily business as though they did not have a care in the world.

Reynolds's news meant that the life style that Logan had become accustomed to was about to be blown apart. The senseless murder of his daughter had almost destroyed him but now this ... the secret was out and men he had believed were long dead were still out there.

Damn and blast his brothers George and James. He knew he should never have involved himself in their business. They were both dead – victims of vengeance attacks after they had betrayed McIntire and others by leading them into an ambush at a bank when all the time the gold they were planning to steal was safely locked up in the vaults of the Springwater Banking and Trading Company.

Here, below where he now stood, was more gold than any man could need but now, according to Reynolds, McIntire and the survivors of that abortive raid were coming to claim it. And claim him, Henry Logan, mayor and respected citizen of Springwater – brother of the traitors. Logan neither knew nor cared how Reynolds got his information but he did know from experience that it was reliable.

Reynolds was a drifter, a loner who gathered information like a dog gathered fleas and it always came at a price – but a price that Logan could readily afford.

He had even used Reynolds to delve into the history of Jim Gannon once the sheriff had started to show an interest in his daughter Kate. It was Reynolds who had supplied the information that Gannon was from a solid Kansas farming family of good character and more than suitable as a husband for Kate to help her forget that no-hope layabout Dan Cameron, whom she had married against her father's wishes.

It was also Reynolds who had tipped him off about the precarious state and problems he would have if he went ahead with his plan to buy into the Brady Stage and Transport Company.

The business had closed even before the opening

of the new railroad and Henry Logan had been saved from making a bad investment.

Sam Reynolds was worth every cent of the money he received but this latest piece of news sent the cold shiver of fear down Logan's spine. What could he do? Where could he run to where he would be safe with his gold. He would have to flee across several states – maybe up north to Wyoming or Montana or west to California – and he would still be looking back in a constant state of fear.

Nowhere would be safe and even if he handed over the gold would these men, hell bent on vengeance, let him walk away?

It was at that moment that another horrifying thought struck him.

If they were so full of hate for the Logan family had one of them already exacted some extra revenge? Had one of them gunned down his beloved daughter while she picnicked at the side of a quiet creek?

Had Clay McIntire – or one of his bushwhackers – killed an innocent woman as part of a hate campaign?

God – would they stop at nothing?

Despite the heat, Logan felt a cold shiver as he reached inside his coat and pulled out a fistful of notes. He counted out the dollar bills and thrust then into Reynolds's hand. He tried to smile but it was a fruitless attempt.

'Thanks, Sam. I'm grateful and if you hear

anything more, well' – he pushed another five dollars towards Reynolds – 'you know where to find me.'

'Sure do, Henry,' the visitor said rising from his seat and moving to leave. 'An' if you don't mind me saying so, I'd be getting myself some sort of protection. From what I hear these men may be after your blood.'

Logan didn't speak as the other man left the room and headed down the outside stairway to the back alley. Nor did Logan see the smug smile on the face of his visitor.

This was the easiest money he had ever earned – and being paid by both sides made it doubly sweet. It was true, Henry Logan had been a good source of income but when a man stops you in the street and tells you he's got a message for the mayor and offers twenty dollars just to deliver it, only a fool would turn that down.

The message had been simple enough: 'Tell Logan that McIntire and his men haven't forgotten and they'll be paying him a visit real soon.' It could have been innocent enough but why would that be worth twenty dollars? And Reynolds was no fool. There was something sinister about the man and his message and, judging from old Henry's reaction, this McIntire's men were not planning on making it a friendly call.

Reynolds mounted up and reached the edge of town before the man in black moved out from behind a bush and waved him to stop. Satisfied that Sam had delivered the message, he handed him his twenty dollars and sent him on his way. Sam Reynolds did not need telling twice. Things were getting too hot around Springwater.

Jim Gannon removed the untouched plate of food from Ike's cell and, without a word, went back to his office desk. Ike had long since given up complaining – the non-appearance of his father doing most to silence him. Gannon, too, was surprised by Clayton's failure to visit the jail and demand the release of his sons. News of their arrest should have reached him hours ago and it wasn't like Jack to sit on his hands when action was called for.

But when the door opened it wasn't Jack Clayton who walked in. Standing in the doorway when Gannon looked up from his paperwork was Henry Logan.

Gannon hadn't seen him since Kate's funeral and although he thought he looked ill then, he looked infinitely worse now. He had the look of a man with the worries of the world pressing down on him.

'Come in, Henry. You look as though you need a drink.'

Logan shook his head but sat in the seat usually occupied by Ned Hilton. 'No thanks, Jim, but I do need your help. Or let's say your advice.'

Gannon waited.

'How much did Kate tell you about the Logan family?'

The sheriff didn't answer straight away. He could tell his visitor that Kate had told him nothing but a man called Matt Cameron had told him a lot. Instead he said simply, 'What was there to know, Henry?'

Logan briefly looked lost for words, as if he was trying to pluck up the courage to say what he had come to say.

Slumping forward in his seat, Logan struggled over where to start. Eventually he said, 'I think I know who killed our Kate, Jim. And I think I am the next on his list.'

Henry Logan had all the appearances of a beaten man as he told Jim Gannon his story.

During the early months of the war the South needed all the weapons they could get their hands on – from whomever could supply them. It could never be said that the Logans were slow to go into the market place – whether it was for women, slaves, money-lending. Or supplying weapons.

They bought up a run-down gunsmith's and turned it into a small arms factory, run on behalf of the Confederacy, mostly by slaves. Using the materials they could beg, borrow or steal, the Logans at first produced side-arms that were substandard and refused by the rebels. So they began to import them from across the Atlantic – made by firms in England – carbines, Gatling guns, repeating-rifles as well as the side-arms they continued to produce in Union City, Tennessee.

Then, like most arms dealers, the Logans got greedy.

The rifles and pistols that had been rejected earlier were eventually filtered in among the imports – with disastrous consequences when they misfired, costing lives among the Confederate soldiers at a skirmish in Obion County in sixty-four.

The Logan Brothers had already bought into the Springwater Banking and Trading Company and put their youngest brother, Henry, in charge, persuading him to use his vaults to hide away their war chest.

Then came their biggest mistake. They betrayed the McIntire crew. George and James Logan had become close acquaintances of Clay McIntire on the former Quantrill man's return from Texas and twice helped him in bank raids earning them more than $20,000.

But the South was losing the war and the Logans' love of the secession states did not extend to giving their lives in the cause.

After moving a stash of stolen Union payroll gold from their own bank to that of their brother up in Springwater, they then set up McIntire and his men for their abortive raid. Six of the bank robbers had been caught but escaped almost at once and although two of them were gunned down in the street while making their escape and another wounded, the others, including McIntire himself, had fled.

Only a few days later another bold attempt to rob the bank had again ended in their leaving empty-handed. But this time they had left the bodies of the Logan brothers hanging from the balcony of their favourite whorehouse. They had been tortured before a bullet was put in their brains. Henry paused in his story, his hands still shaking.

Gannon poured him a whiskey but again the mayor refused.

His voice little more than a whisper, he continued, 'Today I had a visit from a man called Sam Reynolds.'

The name meant nothing to Jim Gannon. And that caused Logan to smile if only briefly.

'Reynolds is a man who hears things. He sells the information and people like me pay him for that.' He resisted the temptation to tell Gannon that he had used Reynolds to spy on him once the sheriff started walking out with Kate.

'He came to tell me that McIntire was going to pay me a visit and it was obvious he didn't mean a social call. Jim, I think McIntire still has enough hate left in him to see off the last of the Logans.'

Gannon walked to the window. Outside, the sun had long since given way to nightfall and only the lights of the distant Nugget Saloon and the lamps of a hotel across the street offered any break in the darkness. Gannon finished the drink he had originally poured for his visitor. This was the second time he had heard the name of Clay McIntire in connection with Kate's death. Matt Cameron had been the first to plant the idea in his head and now the Mayor of Springwater had come up with the same notion.

'What are you planning to do about it, Henry? I can't go out and arrest a man just because you think he might be planning to kill you.'

Henry Logan did not get the chance to answer. Suddenly the door burst open and two men, brandishing pistols, burst into the room.

Startled, Logan cowered back in his seat, while Gannon knew that any move for his gun would have been a mistake.

The first gunman, bigger and older than his fresh-faced companion, barked an order, 'Cell keys! Now!'

Jim Gannon leaned into his desk drawer. So this was how Clayton was going to get his sons out of jail? No crooked judge, no fancy fast-talking lawyer . . . just a simple break-out. Gannon tossed the bunch of keys to the gunman.

'Doin' Jack's dirty work for him, huh?'

The man said nothing, instead throwing the keys to his young companion.

'Get those two out of the back – and be quick.' Then, to Logan, 'You, on your feet.'

Henry Logan made no move. Gripped with fear he *couldn't* move.

'I said on your feet!' the man snapped, gripping the mayor's coat and dragging him from the chair.

Gannon made a move to step in but the jailbreaker swung the gun in his direction. 'Don't even think about it, Sheriff.'

Billy was the first to come running from the cells at the back of the office. He was followed almost at once by the young kid who had accompanied the stone-faced man. Limping alongside and clinging on to the young man for support was Ike.

As the two entered the office he pushed his rescuer away.

'A gun! Give me a gun!' There was rage in his voice and the look of hatred in his eyes as he staggered towards Stone Face. 'I said – gimme a gun!'

'I heard you first time. But my orders are to get you out of here, not to go shooting up the place.'

Ike's features became more contorted with a mixture of fury and pain. 'I owe this bastard for this!' He pointed to his leg wound. 'He ain't gonna get away with it. Give me a gun!'

For an anxious moment Gannon expected the man who had come to rescue the Clayton sons was about to do as Ike said. But he was in charge and Ike would be the one taking orders.

'Either you come now – or I leave you here. To me it don't matter too much.'

Ike looked around the room, hoping to find a weapon, any weapon, lying handily discarded.

There was none.

Desperately, he lunged towards the sheriff. 'I'll kill you, Gannon! By Christ, I'm gonna kill you.'

He spat in Jim's face and then turned to the younger man who had been offering his shoulder as support. 'Get us out of here!'

With Henry Logan quivering like a broken wreck as he was dragged along by the younger rescuer, and Ike leaning on Billy for his support, Stone Face turned towards Gannon.

'Don't think I can count on you to sit here till we're out of town, can I?' Without waiting for a reply, he spun the sheriff around before smashing him over the head with his gun butt.

Gannon slumped to the floor as darkness enveloped him.

The raider looked down at the stricken lawman. 'Sorry about that, Sheriff, but it could have been worse – I could have let that crazy dog have his way.'

NINE

The voice was vaguely familiar and the face was little more than a blur. Slowly the vision returned and with it the excruciating pain.

'Take it easy now,' Cameron repeated, helping Gannon to sit up and lean against his office wall. 'That bump on your head is the size of a fist.'

Gannon groaned and tried to get to his feet. It was a vain attempt and he slumped back into a sitting position.

'They came for the Clayton boys,' he said weakly. 'And they took Henry Logan with them.'

'Was it Clayton?'

Gannon shook his head and immediately regretted it. The pain was almost unbearable.

'Not in person. Two of his men. Never seen them before, an older feller, ugly sort, stone-faced and a young fresh-faced kid. But they must have been from Clayton. Who else would want those two out of jail?'

Cameron wondered the same – and he knew only too well why Logan was involved and why he had been dragged off into the night.

It was Gannon who answered any unspoken question.

'Henry Logan is a frightened man. He came to tell me that he was expecting a visit from somebody you know a lot about. Clay McIntire.' Gannon searched the other man's face for some reaction.

'You told me you and the army believed McIntre was responsible for Kate's death, not the Claytons as I thought,' Gannon said, fingering the lump on his head for the first time.

Cameron helped the sheriff to his chair, perching himself on the corner of the desk.

'You thinking of going after the Clayton boys?'

Gannon nodded. It hurt. 'You offering to help me bring them back?'

Cameron had already decided on that. 'You're gonna need help and I'm as good as you are likely to get. Ned's too young to die fighting the likes of the Claytons.'

Gannon struggled to his feet, staggered for a moment and then slumped back into his chair.

Cameron grinned. 'I think the Claytons can wait until tomorrow. Right now you couldn't chase down a three-legged mule.'

Gannon had to agree. He was in no fit state to

chase after fugitives. And he suspected that Ike Clayton wouldn't be going far. He had enough hate in him to wait around for his chance to carry out his threat to kill Gannon.

As he settled down for a night's rest in one of the cells vacated by the escaping Clayton brothers, Jim Gannon couldn't help wondering about Matt Cameron's interest. And where did Clay McIntire fit in? He was still thinking about this when he dropped into a restless sleep.

The room was as cold as a graveyard and Henry Logan was frightened. He was tied and he had been blindfolded and strapped to a chair. He had been held that way ever since the man with the cold eyes and the young fresh-faced kid had dragged him out of the sheriff's office at gunpoint. He had known then that he was not just an incidental in the escape.

He was as much a part of the plan as the Clayton brothers.

They had forced him on to a horse and for almost an hour they had ridden at top speed deep into the night – the five of them, the Claytons, their two rescuers. And Henry Logan.

Was this the visit that Sam Reynolds had warned him about?

Henry had no sense of time as he sat there in the darkness behind the blindfold, shivering with a mixture of cold and fear.

He got the occasional smell of tobacco; the

muffled sound of voices he thought he recognized and then decided he was mistaken.

He soon gave up his feeble struggle with the ropes that bound him to his chair and fretted over the questions that kept recurring. Who were these men? Why was he here? What did they want? The questions kept coming and Henry had no answers. Except one.

As the fear grew inside him he tried to persuade himself that this had nothing to do with his brothers, their treachery or the gold that was hidden in the vault of his Springwater bank. But he knew differently.

Why else would two men he had never seen in his life drag him out to a godforsaken corner of the county in the back of nowhere, tie him to a chair and leave him in fear for his life?

Suddenly, Henry heard the door open and slam and heavy footsteps cross the wooden floor. They were heading his way.

The newcomer spoke – a harsh, deep-throated voice.

'Men, I'd like you to meet the man who is going to make us all rich for the rest of our lives. This is our benefactor, Henry Logan.'

Logan trembled. He now knew that he would never get out of this alive. He immediately recognized the voice of the new arrival and he knew even before the blindfold was whisked away the face that would be staring down at him. . . .

There was a time early in her marriage when Ruth Clayton would have worried if her husband or stepsons had not come home at night. Not any more. In fact she was more than happy to think and hope that she would never have to worry about any of them ever again.

She had known Jack would side with his eldest son after the incident with the buckshot but the beating and the brutality of his love-making – in his world an attempt to repair the damage she had done to the family – convinced her that she had done the right thing in telling Matt Cameron of her suspicions about Jack and his association with the man McIntire.

Ruth had always believed that Matt was a good man, but their young love was never going to blossom into anything that could last. Even as a raw-boned youth Matt was already mapping out a military career. Unlike his feckless brother Dan – a worthless layabout who married Kate Logan and then expected her father to keep him for life – Matthew had left home at a young age to make his way in the army. They had promised to exchange letters and for a time they kept that promise; they each made solemn pledges that one day they would be together again.

But two things happened to destroy that young loves' dream – the war and the appearance in her life of Jack Clayton.

When the war started to go badly for the South Jack began to question his loyalty to the Confederacy.

He still spent days and weeks away on military duty while Ike and Billy, neither of whom was cut out for ranch work, became bored without their father's company. Even on his brief and rare visits home, Jack was distant and unfeeling. The marriage – her life – was in pieces and nobody seemed to care. The small work-force walked out as a protest against the brothers' idleness and arrogance.

Josh Clarke's small but successful ranch that he had left to his only child, quickly became a rundown shell. So when her husband and sons failed to return after leaving early the previous day, Ruth decided that the longer they stayed away the more she would like it. But as she swept away the dust from the veranda and straightened the discarded furniture, she was surprised to see two riders approaching the house from the main track that led from Springwater. What was it that could be bringing Matt Cameron and Sheriff Gannon to the house?

Ruth did not want to believe what she had just heard, but she knew that it was close to the truth.

It was no surprise that her stepsons had got themselves into more trouble with the law but a jailbreak, and worse, the kidnapping of the town's mayor, would put them on the Wanted list of every law enforcement officer and agency in the state.

'But you say Jack wasn't there? He wasn't involved?' she asked. 'Who then?'

Matt Cameron put a comforting arm around her shoulder, as he had so often in their youth.

'We need your help, Ruth. The two men who broke into the jail and got the boys out and took Henry Logan were not known to Jim here, but we do think that Jack sent them to do the job. Now we've got to find them. Will you help?'

'How can I help you? I haven't seen Jack or his sons since they rode off just after the sheriff came with his young deputy. The brothers went off in a rig and Jack took his horse. I watched them leave from my room upstairs, but I don't know where they were going.'

Jim Gannon interrupted. 'That's when Ned and I picked them up and arrested them. They were heading south from the ranch.'

'But Jack didn't go with them, unless. . . .' It was Cameron who spoke but his voice tailed off almost immediately. Then he surmised, 'Unless he was acting as a decoy to see if they were being followed.'

'That's it,' Cameron snapped with a note of triumph in his voice. 'I followed him but I didn't want to get too close. He spotted me and I lost him.'

Gannon took up the train of thought.

'And he was due to rejoin the brothers at some pre-planned meeting place. When they didn't show he knew something had happened to them. That they had been arrested.'

The two men fell silent, both obviously jumping to the same conclusion. That was how Clayton knew his sons were in jail – and he had planned their escape from his hideaway. But who were the two men who had staged the breakout? And why had they taken Henry Logan with them?

Gannon turned to Ruth. 'Have you ever heard Jack talk about any place south of here? Or friends – maybe army friends – from out that way?'

Ruth shook her head.

'Think!' Gannon urged her. 'Anything you can remember might help us to track them down.'

She was silent for almost a full minute before she eventually said, 'I've never heard Jack talk of anything out that way but I remember Billy once saying that he and Ike were out riding and came across this old town – Cinto, Clinto, something like that – but it was deserted. A complete ghost town. There was nothing there.'

'Calto!' Cameron said, turning to Gannon. 'And can you think of a better place to hide out?'

'You think that's where they'll be?' Ruth was puzzled. 'But why? They can't stay out there for ever?'

Gannon chuckled. 'I don't think they'll be staying there that long, Ruth. They took Henry Logan for a reason and if my guess is right they'll be moving on once they've finished with him.'

'Moving on?'

'I think so, Ruth. You could say that some good will come out of this,' said Gannon pleasantly. 'One way or another I think you've seen the last of your husband and his two sons. They won't be returning to Springwater.'

He turned to Cameron. 'There'll be at least five of them but I don't think they'll be going anywhere right now. I think we've got time to deputize a few men and form a posse. We won't get too many volunteers to hunt down the killer of the Mexican, but when we tell them they've taken the mayor we won't be short of guns.'

Cameron nodded his agreement but as the two men rode away from the ranch, leaving Ruth to hope that Jim Gannon was right, they were going to regret the delay. The kidnappers were already making their plans.

The streets of Springwater were deserted when the four men arrived in town. Stores were closed and the citizens – except for the few still in the Nugget Saloon – had long since locked their doors for the night.

The fresh-faced kid was driving the wagon they would need to haul the gold, the others were riding alongside a frightened Henry Logan.

'Get that thing out of sight!' The order came from Stone Face and the young wagon driver turned into the covering darkness of a side alley.

Logan was trembling as he was ordered to dismount outside the rear of the Springwater Banking and Trading Company. He had been in that state ever since the blindfold was removed and he stared into the faces of the men standing over him.

Immediately he had been taken from the sheriff's office he knew that the day of reckoning he had been dreading had finally arrived. These men had not taken him because he was the mayor of some small Missouri town and now, as he stood outside the rear entrance of his own bank he dared not wonder what the future held.

The stone-faced man who had dragged him out of the sheriff's office now pushed him brutally towards the door.

'Move it. We're in a hurry.'

Henry fumbled for his keys and in the darkness of the alley, he had trouble opening the lock.

'I said move it!' The ugly man was losing what was left of his temper.

'I'm trying. Please, I'm trying.' Henry Logan sounded like a bleating child. He was close to collapse. He had little doubt that these men had orders to kill him once they had entered the vault and removed the gold and emptied the boxes of any riches in Henry's safe keeping.

Even the fresh-faced youth who had helped in the Clayton brothers' breakout would not hesitate to put a bullet in Henry. He had never seen the third man before but he judged on appearances and the man had the look of a hardened killer.

What chance had he of escape? How could an ageing banker held at gunpoint by a cold-eyed killer get away from his captors and call for help?

There was no doubt in his mind that these were the men who had brutally tortured, shot, then hanged his two brothers down in Tennessee; and one of them had killed his daughter. Of that he was sure.

It was that knowledge that gave him strength. Maybe he couldn't escape, but he could die trying. He would not surrender meekly like a lamb to the slaughter and while there was breath in his body he would use it.

One slack moment, one lapse of concentration from his captors was all he would need, but as he opened the door and was pushed into the dark interior of the bank he knew that he would need something approaching divine intervention to come to his rescue – and Henry Logan had never been a man to turn to praying.

He felt the pistol in the small of his back. He was pushed towards the vault, protected by steel bars and a heavy locking system. Again he fumbled with the keys and again he was ordered to hurry.

Then, as the door of the vault swung open, the man holstered his six-gun and went inside. He was immediately followed by the youngest of the trio. The third man had been left outside to keep watch in the alley. Maybe it was the sight of the gold, maybe it was their anxiety to finish the job and make a quick exit but whatever the reason, both men briefly ignored Henry Logan, pushing him against the wall of the narrow corridor.

'Light the lamp,' Stone Face ordered the younger man, 'then help me with this. . . .'

Unnoticed, Henry edged slowly along the corridor keeping his back pinned to the wall.

They were ignoring him. The gold was all that interested them. Slowly, silently, Henry shuffled his way back the way they had come. Before the exit another door led off to the right and into the rear of the trading store that formed the front of the building. Urged on by a combination of survival instinct, fear and the dread that any moment the two men in the vault would notice he was missing, Henry squeezed his way through the cases of supplies that were stacked neatly in piles at the rear of the store. Ahead, the front of the building led out on to Springwater's Main Street . . . and the slim hope of safety.

Terrified of making the slightest sound, Henry eased the key in the lock and held his breath. Then, as if on cue, came a shout from behind. They had noticed he was missing!

Panic pushed him on. Gone now was the need for silence as he slung the door open, dashed out into the street and headed for the semi-security of darkness. Gasping for breath, Henry stumbled along the boardwalk. Would they come after him? Would they risk everything to put a bullet in his back and waken the town? Or would the gold – and their greed – outweigh their boss's demand for revenge?

Henry ran until the darkness devoured him. Every step seemed like a new surge of life but although each one took him further from danger it was only fear that spurred him on and not even the dread of capture could add strength to his legs or more air into his bursting lungs. To reach the saloon he would have to cross the street and even in the darkness that would make him an easy target for the killers.

Stopping to regain his breath, Henry shuffled into a narrow gap between two buildings and strained his ears for any sound of pursuers. There was none.

Had they given up on him to concentrate on the robbery? Surely the gold and the money in the vaults were far more important than revenge for a long-ago conflict? But Henry knew that wasn't the case. They would not hesitate to kill him once the vaults had been emptied.

And he knew there was only one place that could offer any hope of escape . . . Jim Gannon's house. The thought gave him extra strength and he moved quickly out of the narrow alley and up on to the boardwalk that ran along all the buildings on his side of the street.

Edging his way along in the darkness Henry was within sight of Gannon's house when the first bullet hit him in the right shoulder. His desperate attempt to scramble on exposed him to the three robbers heading away from the bank. The next bullet caught him in the hip, spinning him round and sending him sprawling off the wooden walkway and into the dirt.

Another bit into the dust close to his head, spraying it into his eyes while a fourth bedded itself in a wooden post.

Henry Logan lay there as he watched the three men and the gold-laden wagon disappear into the night. He struggled to his feet only to slump immediately to his knees. Just a few yards to go but the pain was agony. He was suddenly cold and as he tried to regain his feet he felt the blood running down inside his sleeve.

He was near total collapse and he had never known such fear.

Was death so close?

Staggering to his feet, Henry made one last push towards the house but, as he reached the wicker gate, he slumped forward with a feeble cry for help.

Inside, Jim Gannon had been wakened by the sound of gunfire and rushed to the door, rifle at the ready. But the sound of racing hoofs fading into the distance told him that he was too late to stop the shooting. Laying his weapon aside he rushed out to help the man slumped over his fence.

It was only when Gannon got the man inside and into the light that he recognized him. He was still alive but there was plenty of blood and he was barely breathing.

Gannon carried him across to a couch, laid him down as gently as he could and tried to make him comfortable. He had enough experience of gunshot wounds to know that Henry Logan's hopes of survival were not good and he needed to get Doc Murray without delay.

But, as he moved towards the door, Henry's feeble, croaking voice, held him back.

'Jim . . . it's too . . . there's something you should know . . . I—'

'Easy, Henry, I'll fetch the doctor.'

'Too late, Jim. I'm not going to make it . . . I—' he spluttered and coughed up blood and his head slumped to one side.

Gannon knew it was too late to save his friend. Doc Murray was no miracle worker and Henry Logan was going to need a miracle to survive. 'What happened, Henry. Who did this?'

'Something you gotta know, Jim' – another spluttering cough, more blood – 'Jack Clayton.'

'I knew it!'

'No, no, you don't understand—' Henry Logan gasped out his last words. 'Jack Clayton and Clay McIntire, they're one and the same man.'

Henry Logan did not live long enough to see his

Springwater Banking and Trading Company burn to the ground – the last act in a man's revenge on an entire family.

TEN

Jack Clayton, alias Clay McIntire, was losing patience. His men should have been back an hour ago. What was so difficult about taking a yellow-livered old man like Logan to his own bank, getting him to unlock the vaults and then setting fire to the place with Logan left bound and gagged inside? He was also losing patience with his eldest son. Ike had spent the day bleating about his injuries, his determination to get even with 'that bastard Gannon' and asking damn fool questions about his life as Clay McIntire.

Clayton also knew he had seen the last of Ruth. Not that she mattered any more but there had been times when they were close.

How much did she know? How much had Ike – or more likely Billy – told her which might mean that she could lead Gannon to them before he had completed his plans to head out West?

Clayton stood on the porch of the abandoned

Calto store, lit himself another cigarette and stared out towards the range of hills in the distance. Beyond them was his ranch, Springwater, and his men and the gold.

Where were they? What could be taking them so long, unless ... he dismissed the thought of betrayal almost before it entered his head. He had trusted his men in the past and they had relied on him. There was no reason to think that things had changed. Even so, he was losing patience.

He threw away his half-finished smoke and stormed back inside the store. Ike and Billy were involved in a heated exchange over a card deal while Wes Laden, his sergeant in the old days, dozed on a chair near the window.

'They're late, Pa,' Ike said unnecessarily. 'They should be back by now.'

Clayton ignored the sneer in his son's voice. Ike was right but he didn't want to hear it. His sons had urged him to lead the raid on the Springwater bank, not to leave it to the kid, Stone-Face and the other man. And maybe they were right. They had ridden together after the war and he had trusted them then. Could he still trust them now? For the first time in his life Clayton began to have doubts. All that gold – it was a temptation to the most loyal of his men.

'What you gonna do, Pa?'

It was Billy's turn but this time Jack answered.

'I'm gonna give them one hour – and then we're

going out there to find them.'

Wes Laden stirred from his seat in the corner and gazed out into the night.

'No need for that. Sounds like they're here.'

Billy jumped up, Ike struggled to his feet and together they went out to the front porch of the store to meet the three men – Stone-Face Frank, the young kid, Jesse, and Morgan ... three men, a wagon and a stash of gold.

A rare smile crossed Clayton's full face. 'No trouble?'

'Naw, easy. An' we picked up a bonus or two.'

'And?' Clayton waited for the rest of the report. 'What about Logan? You did what I said?'

Stone-Face Frank hesitated. 'We ... we finished him like you wanted, and we set fire to his place. It's just that – he tried to escape. We had to gun him down in the street, not kill him in the fire like you wanted.'

Clayton thought for a moment. The humiliation he had planned for the last of the Logans hadn't happened but at least he was dead. His bank, the newspaper offices, his whole company would be reduced to ashes before anybody could stop it. Just like his brothers and his daughter, Henry Logan was history. Dead.

'You saw him die?'

Nobody answered. Clayton repeated the question. Still no answer until the kid, Jesse, said, 'I didn't miss, boss, and neither did Frank or Morgan.'

'But you're not sure? None of you saw Logan die?'

'Leave it, Pa,' urged Billy from the back of the group.

'But if Logan's not dead, this job ain't finished,' Clayton snapped angrily.

'He's dead, I tell ya,' Frank argued. 'We got him. We got the gold. The job is finished.'

Jack turned and went inside. How could he be sure? How could they know that Henry Logan hadn't crawled away to get help?

How could he be sure that Logan hadn't managed to use his last breath to blurt out what he knew . . . that Jack Clayton and rebel soldier Clay McIntire were the same person.

And until he knew for certain, his obsession to destroy the entre Logan family and all they stood for would nag away at his innards. Not even the sight of his men unloading the gold and the cash from the wagon could return the smile to Jack Clayton's weather-battered features.

This was not over.

The flames quickly took hold and Springwater's firefighters lost their battle.

Eventually, they had to draw back, beaten by the heat of the town's finest building being reduced to rubble. It was almost dawn by the time the flames died away and the inferno became just a smouldering mass of furniture and machinery. Slowly the crowds who had left their beds and their saloon cards to help, dispersed and returned to their homes.

Gannon and Cameron, soot-stained and drained of all their energy after spending most of the night fighting the fire, sat across the desk from each other in the sheriff's office while young Ned Hilton poured more of his foul-tasting coffee.

It was Ned who eventually broke the sombre silence with the question, 'So, what we gonna do, Jim?'

Gannon had been thinking about that. 'We'll need more guns, and after working all night on the fire most of the fit men in this town are in no shape to join a posse.'

Matt Cameron stood up and paced the floor.

'We can't waste too much time. Clayton – or McIntire or whatever his real name is – he's not going to hang around too long now that he's got his gold. We've got to go after him.'

Gannon knew the soldier was right. Clayton had already run out on his wife and his next step would be to get out of the state with his sons and whoever was riding with him.

But where would he be heading? Trying to think one step ahead of Clayton and using the ghost town of Calto as a starting point, Gannon guessed that he would ride south maybe through Oklahoma to Texas, or perhaps Tennessee, where he had spent most of his war.

Gannon was still thinking over his next move when a fresh thought struck him; why not make

Jack Clayton come to them?

He turned to Matt Cameron. 'Didn't you say that Clayton – this man McIntire – wouldn't settle until he had got his revenge on all the Logan family?'

'That's right,' Cameron nodded. 'And now that Henry Logan's dead and he's got the gold, he'll be hightailing it out of Missouri on the fastest horse he can find.'

'Mebbe not,' said Gannon quietly. 'Think about it for a minute, Matt. What happened last night?'

Cameron and Ned gave the sheriff a puzzled look.

'It looks to me like Clayton – or some of his men – came into town with Henry Logan as their prisoner to open up the bank, take the gold and whatever else was in the vaults, then kill Logan before they made their escape.'

'That's about it, Jim,' Cameron agreed. 'That's what happened.'

Jim Gannon jumped to his feet.

'But did it? Sure they robbed the bank, took the gold, even set fire to the building before escaping.'

'And they killed the mayor,' Ned chipped in.

'Yeah,' said Gannon eagerly, 'but they don't know that. When they rode off Henry was still alive. He was lying out there in my yard. If you're right about Clayton's obsession with killing off all the Logans, he won't give up till he's sure. What if. . . ?' He hesitated, mulling the plan over in his mind before going on.

'We'll need old Doc Murray and the undertaker to go along with us. We've got to make Clayton think that Henry Logan's still alive.'

Wes Laden didn't take kindly to being the man doing a boy's work. Running errands, even for Clay McIntire, was something that should have been done by that young bully boy Ike, or his sniffling brother Billy.

'They can't be seen in town, Wes,' Clay had said convincingly, 'they're already on the run. The sheriff reckons Ike killed some no-good Mexican. It has to be you, Wes, because nobody knows you in Springwater and I can trust you. Find out if Logan's dead – then we'll move on.'

As he rode alone into the evening twilight, Laden felt the temptation to tell Clay exactly what he wanted to hear . . . that Logan was dead and ready for burial. But he knew from experience that McIntire didn't take kindly to any of his men trying to dupe him.

He could remember the time just after they had left Quantrill down in Texas when Case Jennings had held back on the railroad depot loot and Clay stored it up until the chance came during another raid. He sent Jennings walking into a shower of bullets at another stage station. Laden remembered that it cost Case his life – but it saved the rest of the McIntire crew.

As he dismounted outside the Nugget Saloon,

126

Wes Laden had no intention of becoming the next victim of Clay McIntire's idea of justice. Laden tied his horse to the hitching rail and mounted the steps into the saloon. A piano player was tinkering at some tune he only vaguely recognized and the barman was polishing glasses.

The rest of the place was empty. Not even a card game to join.

He ordered himself a beer and a whiskey and stood at the bar. No doubt the place would fill up later but he didn't have the time to wait for that.

The barman looked bored enough to want to talk to somebody so Laden tried his luck.

'Looks like you had a bad fire down yonder,' he said as an opener.

The barman breathed heavily on the glass he was cleaning and grinned. 'You must be a stranger round here, mister.'

Laden nodded. 'Just passing through. Saw the burnt-out building down the street.'

The barman chuckled. 'Yeah, that was the bank and the newspaper office and the trading company and everything else that mattered here in Springwater.'

'What happened?'

'The place was robbed last night. Three men – they set fire to the place. Don't know exactly what they got way with but they must have been real mad to burn the place to the ground.'

'Anybody . . . er, anybody hurt?' Laden had to be

cautious, not too eager.

'The poor mayor, the guy who owned the place, Henry Logan, he was shot.'

'Bad?'

The barman picked up the whiskey bottle and refilled the stranger's glass.

'Bad enough. We had the doc in today for his usual ... er, medicinal treatment he calls it – whiskey to you and me – and he was telling me about it.'

Wes Laden tried to keep his patience but it wasn't easy. The barman breathed heavily on another glass before wiping it vigorously. Behind him the doors swung open and three cowboys burst in and headed for the bar. The interruption stopped the barman from continuing his story about the previous night's bank raid – and, more important, from letting Laden hear what he wanted to know.

The cowboys tried to make conversation – even invited him to a four hand of poker – but Laden quickly made it known he wasn't interested and they wandered off to annoy the pianist.

Laden ordered himself another beer and decided he would not get a better chance to bring up the shooting of the mayor.

'Have a drink yourself,' he said pleasantly. 'There's nobody around to tell any tales.'

The barman poured himself an extra large whiskey, and rested his elbows on the bar. 'Where were we? Oh, yeah . . . Henry Logan. He got shot up real bad by the robbers when they were riding out. Two, three bullets, the doc said, got him real bad.'

Laden pressed on, 'But he ain't dead?'

The barman drained his glass.

'No, he ain't dead. At least not yet. The doc said he's not got much chance of coming out of it. Seems one of the bullets got him on the throat. He can't speak.

'There's no infirmary closer than a couple of days' ride so he's been bedded down at Doc Murray's house . . . until the undertaker takes him off, I figure.'

Laden had all the information he needed. Clay wasn't going to like it but that was his problem.

The barman moved off to serve a new arrival and Laden drained his glass and headed out of the saloon.

The newcomer ordered a beer.

'Stranger in town, Sam?' he asked the barman.

'Reckon so. Ain't been in here before, that's for sure. Dunno why but he seemed pretty interested in Henry Logan's state of health.'

Jim Gannon moved away from the bar to find a quiet corner to enjoy his beer. The message he had asked the doc to spread around was now on its way to Jack Clayton.

Clayton was angry and when he got angry everybody knew it. Even favourite son Ike kept out of his way as he ranted about the news Wes Laden had brought from Springwater, that Henry Logan was hanging on to life.

Frank, Jesse and Morgan had to bear the brunt of Jack's anger – it was their failure to kill off Logan that had left Clayton with no choice . . . he would have to send them back to finish the job.

The doc's house, from what he could remember, was a small isolated building in a quiet corner of town and the old man lived alone. It should be easy, even for an incompetent trio like them. He knew that in his younger days he would have done the job himself but he had other plans. Daybreak was still a few hours away so there was still time, if they rode hard, to put things right and be back before anybody in that sleepy town was even aware than anything had happened.

Then they would have a surprise waiting for them.

Clayton allowed himself a satisfied grin as he formed the plans in his mind. When they did find out Gannon would come looking for him – and this time he would be ready. He had warned that tin badge to keep out of his business. Before this day was through he was going to regret that he didn't listen to some friendly advice.

The storm set in an hour before dawn in what had already turned into a long watchful night for Gannon and the others. Jim knew that Clayton would waste no time once the report reached him that Henry Logan was still alive and that a raid on Doc Murray's house would take place under the cover of night. And now, as the storm gathered strength and the rain lashed against the windows, Jim Gannon wondered how many they could expect? And would the Claytons be among them? Or would Jack send in some of the gunslingers whom he believed had failed to carry out the killing at the first attempt?

Jacob Potts had left town on the evening stage but Gannon reckoned this had long since passed the need for a judge and jury, and that neither the Clayton brothers – nor their father – would be around to see the inside of a courtroom again.

The three of them – Gannon, Cameron and young Ned Hilton – waited in a shack near the bottom of the rear yard of Doc Murray's house. They had sent the doctor away to a hotel room for his own safety and his house, now empty, was in darkness.

The rain and wind strengthened and Jim was on the verge of calling off the watch when the sound above the noise of the storm told him that the wait had not been in vain.

The whinny of a horse frightened by the flashes of lightning.

Immediately the three men in the shack were alert. Cautiously, Gannon eased open the door and peered into the darkness. He could make out the silhouettes of three men, two had dismounted, one stayed in the saddle. The figures were only fleeting shadows but there was no doubt that these were the men they had been waiting for . . . Clayton's men. But Gannon felt a tinge of disappointment that Jack wasn't with them. Nor as far as he could see, was either of the brothers.

Beckoning the others to follow, Jim edged his way out into the teeth of the wind. Silently, he directed Cameron to his right and signalled Ned to stay back. The young deputy was more than happy to stay crouched in the shack doorway.

The rider who had not dismounted struggled to keep the three horses under control in the raging storm while his two partners moved stealthily towards the house. Once inside they would be trapped and would have to shoot their way out. It would be the chance Gannon needed. He was not looking for a shoot-out – he would rather take all three men alive – but if that was the way it had to be, he had two good men as back up.

But his hopes of a peaceful solution were suddenly dashed – a lightning flash lit up the night sky and before they could move, the lawmen were bathed in blinding light. The element of surprise had gone.

The two men at the house spun round, guns in hand.

The first shot came from the man to Gannon's left but the bullet smashed harmlessly into the fence. Diving for cover, the sheriff returned fire, aiming in the general direction of the first shooter. But he too was hopelessly off target.

One of the gunmen made a dash for his horse but didn't make it, Cameron's bullet hitting him full in the chest to send him spinning backwards into a bush. Badly wounded, he tried to scramble into the safety of darkness but stumbled forward at the first step and crashed into the dirt.

Gannon dodged a bullet from the man on the horse and was about to return fire. But, even as his finger moved to squeeze the trigger, he hesitated.

This was only a kid – and he had a look of terror in his face. Even so, he fired again, aimlessly and at nobody in particular and then spun his horse away from the house. Abandoning the mounts of his two partners, he whipped the horse into a gallop and headed off into the night.

Behind him, Gannon heard another shot and and turned to see the third man, a tall, lean figure, lurch to one side and crash through a fence. To his left, the groans from the first wounded man alerted him to more danger. But there was none, the man was close to death.

Gannon rose to his feet, wiped his face clear of the stinging rain and looked around.

'Cameron? Ned? Anybody hurt?'

Both men stepped out of the darkness.

'Good,' said a relieved Gannon. Turning to his deputy, he said, 'Right Ned, I think you should get the doc from the hotel to see if he can do anything for our friend over there.' He waved towards the wounded man.

'The other's dead,' said Cameron without any hint of sympathy as he holstered his gun. 'But what are we doing about the third man who ran out?'

'We're going after him,' Gannon told him. 'He's sure to lead us to the Claytons . . . and they're the ones we're are interested in.'

'Them – and their gold,' Cameron muttered.

Fear drove young Jesse Fuller on as he battled against the rain. He hadn't waited around but he knew for sure that Frank and Morgan were dead. They had all ridden into an ambush set by that lawman Gannon, the man Clay never shut up about. Well, to hell with Clay, to hell with Gannon. Jesse was getting out – just as soon as he'd got his share.

Oblivious to the dangers he urged his horse on across the treacherous terrain, convinced that the sheriff would be on his tail.

The storm subsided to nothing more than gentle rainfall and slowly the shifting clouds gave way to a clear moonlit night and Jesse urged his tiring horse on to even greater effort. He knew that the clearing skies would make it easier for his pursuers and he was not sure how much of a start he had.

Eventually the silhouettes of the distant hills gave way to the more welcoming sight of the outline of the deserted garrison town of Calto. Soon he would no longer be alone – he would have Clay and those two hothead sons of his and Wes Laden, especially Wes, at his side.

He entered the small silent town at a gallop and headed for the disused store that had been their hideaway since Clay laid out his plans for the bank robbery and the recovery of the gold.

But as he swung out of the saddle and wrapped his horse's reins around the hitching rail, Jesse suddenly felt a pang of unease.

Why was nobody on the porch waiting for him? Somebody should have been on look-out. It wasn't like Clay to leave himself without a guard wherever he was holed up.

Jesse leapt up the step and into the store. It was in total darkness, And it was deserted.

'Clay! Wes!' His voice echoed round the emptiness of the room. Nothing.

Anxiety soon gave way to near panic as Jesse, gun now in hand, raced first into an adjoining room and, finding it empty, out to the back of the building. Again – nothing. No horses, no rig.

Cursing, Jesse went back inside the store, reached for one of the abandoned whiskey bottles and poured himself a large slug, swallowing it in one gulp before slumping into a chair.

The bastards have given me up, he thought. Frank and Morgan are dead and I'm out here in this godforsaken hole while they count their share of the gold. Clay McIntire can rot in hell.

He finished another drink, poured a third and

was still sitting there, almost an hour later and oblivious of anything around him, when a figure appeared in the moonlit doorway.

Jesse turned to see a gun pointed at his chest. He waved the near empty bottle in the direction of the silhouette.

'Come on in, stranger. Have a drink. As ya can see, I'm short of company.'

Gannon hostered his gun. This kid was no threat and he wasn't interested in locking up somebody who would be a danger only to himself until the effects of a bottle of whiskey wore off.

Billy Clayton was worried.

'You sure about this, Pa? I mean, that Gannon ain't gonna come by single-handed – he'll have men with him. And guns.'

Ever since they had left the Calto ghost town and Jack had outlined his plans to finish 'once and for all that interfering sheriff' and headed back to the ranch, it seemed to Billy that they were only asking for more trouble.

'Why don't we just get outta here like we planned to?'

But Clayton wasn't listening. He sat silently in his seat on the ranch porch, ignoring his son's bleating, and staring out into the night. Gannon would come and he would bring guns, and there would be no end to this until he was in the ground. Just like the others.

Billy turned away and went inside the house

where Ike was ranting at his stepmother, threatening her with every punishment he could put his tongue to.

Also in the room, Wes Laden sat drinking coffee and smoking. Wes had no feeling for either of the brothers and he was sure the woman didn't deserve the foul-mouthed abuse she was receiving. But that was her business. And Clay's.

Billy shuffled past him and threw himself into a stuffed chair. He wasn't sure he wanted to be part of this. He had just learned that his father was two men – one of them a soldier fighting for his beliefs with the Confederacy, the other a man called Clay McIntire, a murderer and rebel who had ridden with William Quantrill before forming his own gang. Did Billy want to be part of that?

Restless, he walked over to the stove and poured himself a coffee but discarded it almost immediately. Ike was getting on his nerves; his father wasn't speaking and Wes just sat there ignoring everybody. It was like waiting for death to knock on the door.

Ruth watched her younger stepson pace the room and began to feel sorry for him. Under Ike's influence he had never had the chance of a decent honest life and now that she knew the truth about her husband she realized that it was too late. The night would end in more death and, if she survived, she felt she would be left to bury three members of her family.

Matt Cameron wanted more than revenge and, if he was half the man she suspected, he wouldn't be leaving empty-handed. No matter who stood in his way.

ELEVEN

The sun rose over the eastern ridge, all signs of the previous night's storm gone and the drying dirt sprayed under the hoofs of the two horses.

With Jesse safely locked away in a Springwater cell and Ned having been given his fresh orders, Gannon and Cameron had made their plans. This was now purely personal – no need for innocent townsfolk doing their duty as posse members to get caught up in the gunfire that was sure to follow.

'Clayton won't run,' said Gannon as the pair paused to give their mounts a breather. 'He'll be waiting for us at the ranch.'

'Him and his gun hands,' said Cameron coolly.

Gannon leaned forward and rested his hands on the horn of the saddle. 'No, I think that kid was telling the truth when we locked him up. He said there were only four of them. Clayton, who he knows as McIntire, the two sons and a gun called Wes Laden.

'One of the sons has a gut full of buckshot wounds and one of my bullet holes, and young Billy's no fighter.'

'So that leaves just Clayton and this fella Laden?' Cameron put in.

Gannon had been thinking about that. There was stolen gold involved and unless he was badly mistaken this showdown would turn out to be much more than a shoot-out between the Claytons and the two of them.

As he edged his horse forward he said a silent prayer that Ned would follow the instructions he had left. Everything could depend on it.

The two men rode in silence until they arrived at the gate leading to the ranch. The name Clarke, lying rotting and unnoticed in the dust, was a reminder to Gannon of how things had been before the Claytons came.

Another hundred yards took them within sight of the ranch house and Jack Clayton on the veranda.

'You were right – they are expecting us.' Cameron pulled his rifle from its scabbard, checked its mechanism and did the same with his pistol. 'I guess we won't be offered a cheery welcome.'

Gannon grinned but without humour. He was planning to give Clayton the chance to hand over Ike peacefully, but he knew that was not going to happen. Jack had threatened him with what would happen if he crossed the Claytons. That time had come.

He nudged his horse slowly forward before dismounting. On foot there would be far more chance of dashing for cover if Clayton decided to let the rifle across his chest to do the talking.

But he didn't. He waited for the two men to come within shouting distance before firing a warning shot into the dust a few yards ahead of Gannon's feet.

'That's far enough, Sheriff. And you too, Cameron, you treacherous bastard!'

There was hate and venom in those final words that took Gannon by surprise. He turned to stare at his companion.'He knows you?'

It was Cameron's turn to grin humourlessly. 'We've met before.'

Gannon turned his attention back to Clayton.

'I've got no grievance with you, Jack. Ike's the one I'm after. He killed that Mexican and he's gotta pay for it.'

Clayton spat into the dirt.

'That filthy Suarez! You wanna take my boy for that crooked Mex?'

'You're not forgetting Zeke Bannister, are you, Jack? Remember, it was that Mex who got Ike and Billy off that. Him and that actor you got to play a phoney judge.'

'Yeah. Clever that, don't you think? But you're forgettin' something, Gannon. To take my boy means you gotta get past me. An' I ain't going nowhere. An' I sure as hell ain't lettin' that bastard with you anywhere near any of mine!'

Without another word he raised his rifle and fired. The shot whistled over Cameron's head as he dived for the cover offered by a large boulder to his left. Gannon ducked behind a bush on the other side of the track and could only watch as Clayton, firing at random backed into the house.

There was a long silence before Gannon eventually peered out from his hiding place. The veranda was still deserted.

He called out, 'Matt! You hit?'

'No!'

Hurriedly checking that they were not being watched, Jim raced across the gap to join Cameron.

'Looks like we are going to need some help,' Cameron suggested. 'McIntire's a stubborn old mule.'

But Gannon wasn't listening. He knew all about Jack Clayton – or McIntire – but how did Matt Cameron know so much? And why had Clayton branded him a traitor? Gannon had the feeling that it had nothing to do with the fact that Cameron had sided with the Union during the war. There was more to his hate than just a choice of sides. The pair had crossed paths before . . . but where? And when?

But now was not the time or the place to find the answer.

'Gannon! You still out there? And you, Cameron? Show yourselves!'

The shout from the direction of the ranch house

caught both men by surprise and they spun round.

Clayton was back on the veranda but this time he was not alone.

At his left shoulder was a tall, slim figure who Gannon guessed to be Wes Laden. Behind them were Ike, crouching like a frightened pup as he clutched at his wounds, and Billy, standing even further back as though none of this had anything to do with him. In front of Clayton was Ruth.

Clayton barked an order to Billy who ran from the veranda, around the side of the hosue, reappearing a few minutes later with three horses and a loaded rig.

'They expecting us to let them ride out of here?' Cameron queried as Clayton pushed his wife down the steps of the porch.

'Maybe Jack's found a decent bone in his body after all and he's sending his wife somewhere she'll be safe,' Gannon scoffed.

That was the last thing on Clayton's mind. His wife was his passage out of there. Gannon was not the sort of man who would risk a shoot-out if a woman was in danger and as long as Ruth was close by there would be no gun play.

He would have given a lot to send Cameron to meet his maker but not at the risk of losing the gold. As for Gannon, he'd put his woman, Kate Cameron, in the ground so that was satisfaction enough unless the sheriff turned out to be more of a problem than just a threatening badge. If Ike and

Billy wanted to pay him back for caging them twice that was their business. He was still thinking about his next move when the first shot came. And then the scream.

He spun round to see Billy clutching his shoulder as he staggered against the house wall.

Crouching, Ike returned fire but his bullets passed aimlessy wide of a target he couldn't even see. Shouting abuse, Clayton knocked his son off balance.

'Wait till you can see what you're shooting at, you crazy young fool!' he snapped.

'But, Pa! They got Billy!'

Clayton looked across at his younger son. He was crouching in a corner, the pain from his shoulder wound doubling him over. He turned, grabbed his wife's arm and threw her towards his injured son.

'See to Billy,' he snapped. Then, 'Wes, you and Ike hold fire until I say different.'

'What you gonna do, Clay?'

There was a long silence as Clayton weighed up the possibilities. If it came to a straight shoot-out he had no doubt that Gannon and Cameron could keep them penned in for as long as they needed.

Eventually, he holstered his six-shooter. 'I'm going out there to talk to them.'

Ike gasped, 'Now who's the crazy fool? They'll gun you down for sure.'

'Thanks for worryin', son, but I don't plan to give them much of a chance to do that. Ike, take over from Ruth and look at Billy's shoulder.'

He reached out and grabbed his wife's arm. 'Change of plan, my dear. You're comin' with me.'

Pushing her forward, he drew his gun and stepped out from the cover of the veranda.

'Sheriff! Cameron!'

His harsh shout stirred the two men from their hiding place behind the knot of rocks. The sight of Jack Clayton holding his wife as a hostage and shield, his gun placed close to her temple, sickened Jim Gannon.

'Let her go, Jack. She's not part of this. It's between us.'

'Ride out, Gannon – and take that treacherous rat with you.'

'We're going nowhere – not without Ike and Billy!'

They were still shouting at each other across the stretch of open land that separated them when Ike's thinly-veiled patience finally snapped. But again his bullet did no damage other than disturb the dust well wide of Matt Cameron's feet.

Gannon and Cameron scampered back to the safety of the rocks while up at the house, Clayton shouted obscenities at his son.

For a long spell there was silence between the two sides as Gannon and Cameron waited for Clayton's next move. It came when he fired a shot to draw their attention.

'You still out there, Gannon?'

'I'm here, Jack – you coming in peaceful?'

'My boy needs a doctor – he's bleeding bad!'

Gannon thought for a moment. He had expected Clayton and his men to try to shoot their way out but the bullet in Billy's shoulder had changed that. Or had it? Was Clayton hatching some scheme?

'Don't trust him, Jim,' Cameron hissed. 'He's worse than a rattler.'

But Gannon wasn't listening. Peering out from behind the rocks he watched Ruth and Ike kneeling over the stricken figure of Billy. Even from such a distance it was obvious that the youngest Clayton was in a bad way.

'Jack!' Gannon called. 'Here's what you do. Get Billy in the rig – Ruth can drive him into town to get the doc to see to him. You, Ike and your hired gun can stay.'

'He'll bleed to death, Gannon! He can't take a ride in a rig. I need to get the doc out here to see to him.'

'Forget that, Jack. Besides, if Billy's as bad as you say, by the time the doc gets here it'll be too late.'

More silence.

Matt Cameron was getting restless.

'Look, Jim. We can't just sit here doing nothing. Just waiting.'

Gannon checked his guns for the third time. 'Any suggestions? Remember, it was your bullet that hit Billy and he's hurt bad. To get to a doctor they've gotta come past us. It won't be too long before Jack cracks. He won't see his boy bleed to death.'

Cameron sighed, a sign of his desperation to convince the lawman that he was badly misjudging the man he knew as Clay McIntire.

'Jim – I don't want to tell you how to be a sheriff, but how much do you know about Clay McIntire?'

'Other than what you've told me and that he's known around these parts as Jack Clayton, not much. But what about you, Matt? You seem to know a helluva lot more than you're telling.'

'No, er, it's only by reputation and that he's a mean no-heart who would leave his own mother to the wolves if it helped him.'

Cameron was lying. Gannon knew that. But why? What was he hoping to gain?

But Jim said nothing and was still trying to figure out his next move when any decision was taken out of his hands.

Just as he had expected, Clayton's patience snapped. He wasn't going to sit around and watch his son's life ebb away.

In a moment of madness Jack had given in to Ike's call to shoot their way out of trouble and at the sound of galloping hoofs, Gannon spun round behind the rocks and his first sight was of three riders charging towards him, their guns at the ready. Levelling his rifle, Jim took aim at the nearest, squeezed the trigger and then ducked behind the rocks.

He did not see Wes Laden spin from the saddle and crash into the dust when the sheriff's bullet ripped into his chest.

The Claytons – Jack and Ike – opened fire but Gannon escaped when a bullet ricocheted off a rock before embedding itself in the trunk of an already dead tree.

Behind him, Gannon heard Matt Cameron curse as another shot scorched his hand.

Ike yelled another of his favourite obscenities and expertly dismounted from his frightened horse and dived for the cover of a bush. He fired again. Blindly.

'You hit, Matt?' Gannon waited for a response. None came. 'Cameron?'

He tried again but there was still no reply. Then, just as he was beginning to wonder if one of the Clayton bullets had finished off his sidekick another burst of gunfire followed.

Ike screamed and Gannon somehow knew it was the scream of death. Cameron had worked his way around the cluster of rocks on to a raised level giving him a clear view to fire the killer shot.

Across the narrow strip of dusty road, Jack Clayton looked on in horror as his son hurtled forward, crashing into the hollow that ran between the clumps of greenery. For the first time in his life Jack Clayton prayed.

'God! No! Please. Not Ike!'

'Give it up, Jack! Ike's gone.' Gannon's shouted

offer broke the spell, bringing Clayton back to the reality. Rising to his feet, he staggered out into the open, spraying rifle bullets in every direction. He was a standing target but suddenly confusion reigned as the gunfire seemed to come from all around.

Then Gannon stood and watched as Jack Clayton, six-gun in one hand, empty rifle in the other, slumped to the ground.

Jim Gannon holstered his gun and hurried forward. Kneeling down over the almost lifeless body of the man he had come to arrest, he watched helplessly as the man struggled to hang on to the remaining moments of life.

'You're a fool, Jack,' Gannon whispered leaning over the dying man.

Clayton coughed blood but managed to splutter, 'No bigger fool than you, Gannon. He's taken you for—'

Jack Clayton breathed his last at the same time that the roof of Jim Gannon's world crashed in on his head.

TWELVE

The ropes were knotted tightly around his wrists and his arms had been forced behind the back of the upright wooden chair.

He opened his eyes to find that he was in a large room grandly furnished, though the stuffed chairs and sofas were fading through a combination of age and neglect.

He knew almost without thinking that he was in the main living-room of the Claytons' house. The last thing he remembered was staring down into the unseeing eyes of Jack Clayton and the dying man trying to croak a warning. . . .

Now his head ached from the vicious blow of an unseen attacker.

Unseen, but not unknown, and the first voice he heard after regaining semi-consciousness confirmed that.

'He's coming round.'

It came from behind his head but there was no

mistaking the sound of Matt Cameron – the man he knew had slugged him and, presumably, dragged him into the house and lashed him to the chair.

He came round to stand over his prisoner.

'Sorry about this, Jim, but so much gold can do things to a man.'

Painfully, Gannon tried to move his head so that he could call over his shoulder. 'And to a woman, I suspect,' he said quietly but with every confidence that he would be right.

Cameron grinned.

'You hear that, Ruth? I reckon you can come out now. No point in hiding away from our smart sheriff any longer.'

Ruth Clayton came into view. She no longer had the appearance of a frightened woman wondering when her next beating would be coming. She had cleaned up, put on a fresh dress and she was smiling.

'I guess you've made sure the others are dead, but where's Billy?' Gannon asked for something to say.

'We did our best for Billy,' Ruth said, and there was even a tinge of regret in her voice. 'He wasn't a bad person – he just came from a bad family.'

'So, that leaves only us,' Cameron said lightly. 'And, to be honest, Sheriff, you're a bit of a problem.'

'Glad to hear it,' Gannon answered. 'What next?'

'I think we'll be leaving you here when we go,'

Ruth told him. 'After all, you've done us no harm and we're not cold-blooded murderers.'

No, just thieves and hot-blooded killers, Gannon thought, but remained silent.

Eventually he said, 'What got you involved in this Ruth? Don't tell me your old love fanned the flames when he rode into Springwater?'

Cameron and Ruth looked at each other and came to a decision. Jim Gannon deserved to know the whole story. He couldn't touch them now and they would be out of the state, maybe well on their way to California by the time he got round to looking for them.

'Do you know, Sheriff, it was all down to a case of mistaken identity,' Cameron said. 'If I remember, you even had an attack of that yourself when I walked into your office.'

Gannon recalled how he had been shocked by the likeness between Matt Cameron and the man in the pictures on Kate's piano . . . her husband Dan.

'Most people, including his wife's father, Henry Logan, reckoned my brother Dan to be not much more than the town idler so when he was gunned down one night after another of his bar-room brawls nobody, except maybe his wife, missed him, or even cared. The sheriff put the shooting down to a quarrel over a card game and the killer would be long gone before he could round up enough men to form a posse.

'Dan wasn't killed by a gun-happy gambler,

Sheriff. He was killed because he looked too much like me.

'Bad luck for Dan – and lucky for me – the man Clay McIntire sent to do the killing got it wrong. Maybe it was the one lying outside with a bullet in his chest, which is some sort of retribution on Dan's behalf.

'Clay's lust for revenge against the Logans after that failed raid in Tennessee got the better of him.'

Gannon looked up. 'You were there? The night the Logan brothers turned on Jack and his men?'

Cameron chuckled. 'Sure, I was there. And I ain't ashamed to say that I was one of those who turned him in. Me and the Logans. You see, Sheriff, Clay McIntire was hungry for more power. He wasn't going to be part of any Southern surrender and he was planning to use the gold to buy himself a new private army. It was a crazy idea and we all knew it but Clay was never one to see sense.

'After the failed raid on the Tennessee bank and the loss of two of his men, I knew he would be eaten up with the idea of revenge against those he thought had crossed him – me, the Logans, and anybody connected with the Logans.

'When I heard that Kate had been killed it made sense that he would think there was only old Henry left and he was the one who was holding the gold.'

Cameron paused, putting his arm around Ruth's shoulders.

'So there was me, Clay and whoever else was still

riding with him. Wes Laden would have done anything for Clay – like I said, he was probably the one who gunned down my brother – so it was a safe bet he would still be around. Then there were his two sons. I'd never met them but I'd heard a lot from their old man. Ike was like his father in many ways, quick and hasty with a gun, while Billy wasn't exactly the kind of son his father was looking to rear.

'Even so, the odds were not in my favour. Four against one – I didn't like my chances. I needed help.

'Ruth here was more than willing. Like I said at the time I came into your office, we have a history.

'The day you saw us talking in the street, that wasn't an accidental meeting. We had been seeing each other pretty often. Clay talked too much when he had had a drink. So Ruth listened and reported back to me.

'But that wasn't enough – I needed some more help. Especially guns. That's where you came in, Sheriff. With the law on my side I knew I'd have a better chance so I told you as much of the truth as I needed you to know. The bit about me being a US soldier on a spot of private duty was something I just threw in to get you on my side.

'And it worked,' he added smugly.

Gannon was left to guess the rest.

Posing as a US soldier assigned to the job of recovering gold bullion stolen while it was being

154

transported to pay Union troopers fighting in the South, Cameron had come up with a story that sounded reasonable enough to Gannon. It was the first he'd heard of a reb called Clay McIntire, any missing gold or a feud with the Logans.

But Jim Gannon had never been the trusting sort when it came to strangers and their stories or when they turned up at convenient times. And there was something that didn't ring quite true about Cameron's claim that he was still trying to solve the mystery of who killed his brother.

Cameron broke into his thoughts. 'The Claytons are all dead, I've got the gold. Now I just have to figure out what to do about you, Jim.'

He spoke as though he was merely thinking aloud and another life was of no real concern.

Gannon wrestled with the ropes but only succeeded in increasing the pain as they dug deeper into his wrists.

Ruth came back into the room and stood next to Cameron, eyeing up their prisoner before she said, 'We can leave him here, Matt. We're not cold killers and somebody will find him soon enough but we'll be long gone.'

Cameron thought about that and then said, 'What would you do, Jim? Think I should listen to Ruth here and just ride out? Or maybe get myself some extra time by putting a bullet in you? Must admit, that idea is starting to appeal. Can't really see why I should have to spend my life worrying that you'll turn up unexpected at my back some day.'

Gannon glanced at Ruth. He could tell by the expression on her face that she hadn't been expecting this.

'Don't talk like that, Matt, let's be going.' She grabbed his arm but he shrugged himself free and turned to face her. His eyes, shining with good humour only seconds before, were now cold. His face was hard and hostile.

'Don't tell me what to do, Ruth!' he snapped. 'I've come this far – I'm not going to let some small town lawman get in my way.'

Shocked at the quick change of mood, Ruth stepped backwards.

'He's no threat to us, Matt. The rig's all loaded up with everything. We can be gone and out of the state by nightfall.'

But Cameron's spirits had changed dramatically. He was no longer the personable soldier she had chosen to be part of the betrayal of her husband. As she stood there in silence she felt herself wondering if there was so much difference between the two men. Was it about to happen all over again?

Jack had been charm itself during the early days although she was not sorry he was dead she was no longer certain that the man at her side was any more likely to bring her lasting happiness. Indeed the answer came to her almost before the notion had a chance to form in her mind.

Cameron pushed her away from him, sending

156

her tumbling to the floor and Gannon could only look on helplessly. Straining at the ropes was doing no good.

'I say when and where I go and I say who goes with me.' Cameron spat out the words. Then, as if speaking to himself, he went on, 'Why do I need you? Why do I need anybody else? All that gold out there belongs to me. It can buy me any woman I want.'

He sneered at Ruth cowering in the corner. Laughing almost hysterically he turned to face Gannon. 'What do you think, Sheriff? Think I should finish her off too – leave you both here, huh?'

But Gannon wasn't listening. Instead, he was staring past Cameron and into the open doorway leading out on to the veranda at the front of the house.

Ned had not let him down. He had done exactly as he had been told and he stood there with one man on either side of him. All three were pointing their guns at Matt Cameron's back.

'I think, Matt,' Gannon said quietly, 'you should forget all about gold and California and start thinking about what the inside of a jail will look like for the next twenty years.'

Jim Gannon made his way out of the courtroom and along the sunbaked street towards his office. Unlike the last time, he felt no bitterness, only the satisfaction of seeing a chained prisoner being loaded aboard a barred wagon on his way to the state penitentiary.

Matthew Cameron had had no phoney judges or crooked witnesses to get him out of the hole he had dug for himself but his demeanour throughout the trial had been that of a man without a worry in the world. He had even offered Gannon the occasional smile of friendship in an attempt to influence the judge, but any defence had fallen apart with the evidence of Ruth Clayton. It was close enough to the truth to persuade the jury that Matt Cameron was guilty as charged.

Now, as Jim watched the wagon with its prisoner roll out of town, he felt that the time was right to remove his badge for the last time.

There was a visitor waiting for him as he entered the sheriff's office. Ruth Clayton was sitting in his chair and at her feet was a travel bag.

She stood up as Gannon entered. Ned shuffled out of the room.

'I just called in to say goodbye – and thank you.'

Gannon removed his hat, unbuckled his gunbelt and returned the smile.

They had got to know each other a lot better since Cameron's arrest. She had lost the hunted look of a woman in distress and their developing friendship had even helped him in his attempt to get over the death of Kate, gunned down, he now knew, by Jack Clayton.

'Thanks? For what?'

'For keeping me out of prison, I suppose. You played down my part in what happened.'

'And you helped me to put Cameron away so we're even,' Gannon said helpfully. 'You travelling?' He nodded towards the bag.

'I've sold the ranch to Will Barnes – he's already got the spread next door and he gave me a fair price – and I thought I'd head back to Jefferson City. They always said if I ever wanted to go back there'd be a job waiting for me.'

There was a slight pause before she added, 'You got any plans to stay around?'

'Nope. Early tomorrow I'm heading up to Kansas. I've done my share of fighting the bad guys. I'll leave Springwater in Ned's hands.'

There was another brief silence before a shout from outside signalled that the Jefferson stage was about to leave. Gannon reached down for the travel bag just as Ruth did the same. Their hands touched and for a brief moment they looked directly into each other's eyes.

Then the moment passed and Jim lifted the bag and led the way to the door, helping Ruth to climb aboard the stage.

Two other passengers joined her and the driver loaded up the bags and trunks, securing them before climbing up to his seat.

Jim stepped back on to the boardwalk and waved a final farewell to Ruth – again their eyes met and it was only when he turned away that Gannon started to wonder what might have been. . . .

Back in the office, Ned had returned from the rear of the building with a mug of his undrinkable coffee which he placed on the sheriff's desk. Gannon chose to ignore it.

Instead, he removed his badge, opened his drawer and was about to throw it in when he saw the package.

Ned noticed his frown. 'Mrs Clayton left that for you. Said you'd understand.'

Gannon tore away the paper. There was a note inside. It read: *Thanks again for eveything, Jim. Don't think the government are going to miss one or two of these little ones, do you? Ruth Clayton.*

Gannon smiled as he weighed the small gold bars in his palm. So Ruth Clayton had got out of her loveless marriage with something after all.

He had no idea how much she had managed to smuggle away into her travel bag but suddenly, Jefferson City seemed to be far more appealing than the plains of Kansas and work on the family farm.